OTHER BOOKS BY WILLIAM POST

The Mystery of Table Mountain

The Miracle

A Call to Duty

Gold Fever

The Blue Ridge

A Doctor by War

Inner Circles

The Tides of War

The First Crossing of America

The Evolution of Nora

Darlene

The Gray Fox

Captain My Captain

Alaskan Paranormal

Some Boys from Texas

The Law and Alan Taylor

A New Eden

The Riflemen

A Soldier and a Sailor

Kelly Andrews

Sid Porter

A Ghost Tribe

Lost in the Ukraine

A Change of Tradition

Lost in Indian Country

A Promise to a Friend

A Trip to California

Pure Love

A Stranger to Himself

Hard Times

The Wrong Place at the Wrong Time

The Gathering of a Family

The German War

Pure
Love

William Post

authorHOUSE®

AuthorHouse™
1663 Liberty Drive
Bloomington, IN 47403
www.authorhouse.com
Phone: 1 (800) 839-8640

Published by AuthorHouse 08/22/2017

ISBN: 978-1-5462-0495-4 (sc)
ISBN: 978-1-5462-0494-7 (e)

CONTENTS

Preface vii

Chapter 1 Pure Love.. 1
Chapter 2 Kyle Allen 16
Chapter 3 Life On The Farm... 29
Chapter 4 A Family And Tragedy..................................... 36
Chapter 5 Trouble From Chicago 48
Chapter 6 The Escape... 58
Chapter 7 Mrs. Thorton's Boarding House............................ 67
Chapter 8 The Revenge 76
Chapter 9 San Francisco 84
Chapter 10 To California 94
Chapter 11 A Career Change... 106
Chapter 12 The Reunion... 118
Chapter 13 The War And More 127
Chapter 14 A Gun Battle.. 133
Chapter 15 The Korean War 142
Chapter 16 Paul Drake's War 154
Chapter 17 The Appearance Of Kim................................... 164
Chapter 18 The Trip 176
Chapter 19 The Move 181
Chapter 20 The Vietnam War 192
Chapter 21 The Return Home 203

PREFACE

This is a story of two children who lose their parents to the Spanish flue that killed hundreds of thousands of American during and after the First World War. They met at a satellite orphanage in Chicago. The traumatic way they came together brought a love so deep that it superseded the love that anyone can have for another. It was deeper than the love a mother has for her baby or the love a father has for a devoted son or the love a young girl with her first boyfriend.

They pretend to be brother and sister so they could sleep together and nothing would be thought of them being together constantly.

They adopt parents in a unique way. Their adopted father is a key part of their lives. He loses the children when a gangster kills their adopted mother. They disappear as the boy won't chance the life of his true love, even if it means losing their adopted father.

Some of their actions and wording are graphic, but realistic. The story goes from the mid nineteen-thirties, through the Vietnamese war.

This story illustrates what love can be when two people are completely devoted to one another as these two. They look at what they can do for one another and never condemn each other as their love supersedes that.

I would like the reader to see other books I have written shown above. I have several genres to choose from. My flagship is the first book I wrote, *The Mystery of Table Mountain*. It is followed my two books that take the main character from nineteen through his entire life.

I have written several books with Germany as a central setting. Many of my books are about the cowboy era and the Civil war. Check my website to see the covers of several of my books. **novelsbywilliampost.com** Or you can simply google, **William Post, author.**

CHAPTER 1

Pure Love

In 1918 the Spanish Flu inundated America. Thousands died. In North Chicago, although several years later, Alan Reclin lost his parents and sister to the Spanish Flu. His sister, Lee Ann, had been eight, and had always been sickly. Alan read to her and told her stories. She would look at Alan and tell him how much she loved him. There was such sincerity in her eyes that it nearly made Alan cry. Losing his folks was terrible, but losing Lee Ann devastated him.

Alan was only twelve and had no place to go, because his parents had immigrated to America from England. His father had lost his job as he was unable to work. The family had used up all their assets paying for doctors, nursing and food while they were sick. Before Alan's father died, he told Alan about a tin box he kept in the attic. He told him to make sure he took that with him as he knew Alan would be put in an orphanage. Alan found the box and it contained five, twenty dollar gold pieces and fire silver dollars. Alan knew that someone would insist on looking into the box which also contained several letters, keepsakes and his birth certificate.

He had a wool coat that had a hole in one of the pockets. He knew he could put the money in that pocket and the money would go down into the lining of his coat, so no one would know the money was there.

Alan was put in a private orphanage with nine other children ranging in age from eight to twelve. He was the oldest at twelve years old. The home was financed by the state of Illinois as the state orphanages were all full, so they had private homes taking in children who had no place to go. Nearly all the children had lost their parents to the flu.

Mrs. Gordon owned and ran the home where Alan was sent. She was strict, as she had to be. She had two women helping her, but she laid down the rules. As she did not believe in corporal punishment, she had another method that was worse than beatings. She would lock the children in the basement overnight with no lighting. As the children were still young, this was a terrible thing.

The first day Alan was at the home, he was introduced to the children. One of them was an eight year-old girl named Betty Sue Aster. She looked a lot like Lee Ann. Even her mannerisms were like Lee Ann's. She looked at Alan, and held her eyes on his for sometime, and there was an immediate understanding. Alan could tell she was scared and broken hearted after losing her parents. He could just imagine Lee Ann facing life with no one, so it pulled his heart strings.

Betty Sue reminded Alan of a rabbit he once had. Its mother was taken away. The poor thing trembled so, that Alan picked it up and held it for a long time until the rabbit quit trembling, and was warmed by Alan holding it.

The next day Mrs. Gordon gave the children the instructions and rules. It was summer so there was no school. However, Mrs. Gordon knew the children must be kept busy. She gave everyone chores. Each one was to make their own bed and make it correctly. Betty Sue had never made her bed, and was not good at stretching the sheets tight and tucking in the blanket like Mrs. Gordon demanded. She was the youngest and couldn't do many of the things that were demanded of her.

At supper one night she broke a glass and spilled water on the table. This was the end of Mrs. Gordon's patients. She told Betty Sue, she would spend the night in the basement. Betty Sue was terrified of the dark. Alan knew that it would be terrible for her. He waited until Mrs. Gordon returned from the basement where she left Betty Sue, then turned to the boy next to him, and gave him a hard shove right in front of Mrs. Gordon.

She said, "Alan you will join Betty Sue in the basement tonight."

It was just what Alan wanted. Betty Sue was already in the basement, and he knew she was scared.

Betty Sue saw the light in the doorway and Alan coming down the stairs before the light of the doorway turned to darkness again. When Alan reach Betty Sue, she came into his arms. She was trembling all over. It immediately reminded Alan of the rabbit he once owned, whose mother was taken away.

He held Betty Sue and said, "It's okay now, Betty Sue, I've got you, and will keep you safe."

She said, "Oh, Alan I am so scared I thought I might die."

"You won't die now, Betty Sue, because I'm here and always will be. I'll see that you are never scared again if I can help it."

She clung to Alan tightly, and they both cried as Alan was reminded of Lee Ann. Alan said, "I will be your mother, father and brother all in one, Betty Sue, and keep you safe forever. She had now quit crying and the trembling began to wane.

Nearly fifteen minutes passed before Alan said, "Let me light a match, Betty Sue. I remember they had candles down here. I was sent by Mrs. Gordon to fetch a jar of preserves and took notice of the basement's continents."

Betty Sue reluctantly let him go as he struck a match. He said, "I swiped these matches from the kitchen because I knew sooner or later you or I would be put down here. I knew you would be scared all alone in the dark."

"You did that just for me, Alan?"

"Sure." Alan then located a couple of candles and lit them. He then turned to Betty Sue and asked, "Are you hungry, Betty Sue?"

"Oh, yes, and thirsty, too."

"There are some canned peaches in jars along the back wall. We can drink the juice, and eat the peaches." Alan found the peaches, and they just drank from the jars and ate the peaches.

Betty Sue smiled at him as she drank the juice, and ate the peaches.

Alan said, "I had a sister just your age and you remind me of her."

"Where is she now, Alan."

"She's with Jesus. The flu took her. I have missed her very much. You remind me of her, Betty Sue. The first time I saw you, I noticed you had many of her mannerisms. I think that is why I love you."

"You love me, Alan?"

"Sure, neither of us have any family, so we will be a family, if it is okay with you."

"Oh, yes Alan. I wish we were married so we could sleep together every night and never be apart. Married people always sleep together."

"Well, if I am to be your brother, we can't get married, but that doesn't mean I love you less."

"Nor me neither, Alan. I have never loved anyone like I love you."

"We mustn't let the others know, Betty Sue, or they might try to keep us apart, so don't tell anyone."

Betty Sue said, "I see what you mean. It will be a secret between just the two of us. Hold me again, Alan. I feel so safe when you hold me. I love you so much I wish I could stay in your arms forever."

After that night everything went okay for several weeks. Alan and Betty Sue spent some time together, but not that much. However, they found time to be together each day.

During that month Mrs. Gordon hired a handyman, named Lyle Edwards. She had bought two cows to supply the children with milk. Lyle was put in charge of caring for them and milking them. Mrs. Gordon asked Alan to assist Lyle in milking the cows. She knew from experience that if someone was needed, you needed a back up. If Lyle should become sick or not come to work, Alan could fill in.

Lyle instructed Alan how to milk a cow, and soon Alan was milking one and Lyle the other. Alan told Betty Sue about the milking. She wanted to watch him, so Alan asked Mrs. Gordon if Betty Sue could come with him. He assured Mrs. Gordon that Betty Sue would be helpful, so she was allowed to go with him.

Lyle didn't like Betty Sue, as she was constantly asking questions. He was in a bad mood one morning as the three went to milk the cows. Betty Sue and Alan opened the gate to go into the milking area. Lyle was a few steps behind them. Lyle stopped to light a cigarette, and one of the cows saw the opening of the gate and bolted toward it, knocking Lyle down. This infuriated Lyle, and he yelled at Alan.

Alan said, "You were at the gate, it wasn't my fault."

This further infuriated Lyle and he swung his fist at Alan knocking him to the ground. He then jumped on him and began hitting Alan, who was pinned to the ground by Lyle's knees.

Betty Sue saw an axe handle on the ground that was in front of her. She picked it up and swung it at Lyle's shoulder with all her might in an effort to get Lyle off of Alan. Instead of hitting his shoulder the blow went to Lyle's head, and he was knocked unconscious.

Betty Sue looked at Lyle and asked, "Is he dead?"

Alan felt his pulse and said, "No, he's just unconscious. However, we had better get Mrs. Gordon, she'll know what to do."

Mrs. Gordon saw Lyle lying on the ground with a huge lump just above his ear. She said, "What happened?"

Alan told the story as factually as it happened.

6

Betty Sue said, "I didn't intend to hit him on the head, I swung at his shoulder, but I missed and hit his head."

Both Alan's eyes were blacked and his nose was bleeding. Lyle was a foot taller than Alan, and outweighed him by fifty pounds.

Mrs. Gordon was aware that something had to be done or she might be held liable. As the state had put a telephone into the home, she called the person at the main orphanage that supervised her operation.

The supervisor, a Mr. Alfred, said, "I had better call the police as Mr. Edwards may file a complaint."

By the time a detective arrived, Lyle was awake, but had a terrible headache. The detective heard all three stories. Lyle tried to lie about who hit whom, but the evidence of Alan's black eyes were undeniable. Mrs. Gordon followed the detective and Mr. Alfred outside away from the children.

Mr. Alfred looked at the detective and asked, "What should be done?"

The detective said, "If the children are taken to a new facility, I don't think anything will come of it. Mrs. Gordon, do you have a place to keep the two children away from the others, until Mr. Alfred can make arrangements to move the children?"

"Yes, I have a basement to keep them in. What about Mr. Edwards?"

"I see you need him to milk the cows, so I suggest you keep him, but don't let him mix with the children. Can you do that?"

"Yes, I will tell him to just leave the milk pails on the back porch."

"Then it's settled," the detective said.

After the detective left, Mrs. Gordon said, "The detective said to take Betty Sue and Alan away, Mr. Alfred. I hate to separate those two, as they have a natural attachment for one another."

"All the more reason to separate them. There might be more trouble if they are together." he replied.

Mrs. Gordon and Mr. Alfred were unaware that both Betty Sue and Alan were listening at the door. When Mrs. Gordon turned to go in, they both went back into the living room as if they were there all the time.

After supper that night, Mrs. Gordon said, "Alan I want you and Betty Sue to get your things together. You will be sleeping in the basement tonight. I had Mrs. Lambert make you pallets down there. You will be alright. I'll leave a lamp for you.

Alan and Betty Sue got their things together. Alan had his knapsack and Betty Sue had a cloth sack. They carried everything they had to the basement and Mrs. Gordon had a lamp and went ahead of them. She lit the lamp in the basement. She showed them where they would sleep, then turned and left.

Alan knew why they were there, but asked, "Why are we in the basement, Mrs. Gordon?"

"The detective asked that you be separated from the other children. You will be going to another facility tomorrow."

"Will we be going to the same facility?"

"No. Mr. Alfred thought it best to separate you two. He thought if you stayed together, more trouble may occur. Now go to sleep. I'll see you in the morning at breakfast."

Betty Sue said, "I can't live without you, Alan. Can't you do something?"

"Yes, I can, Betty Sue. We can run away. It will be hard, but we can do it. It's the only way we can stay together."

After ten that night, when all were in bed, Alan lifted a basement window and they were able to squeeze out of it with there things. Alan had found a cloth valise and they put everything they had in it.

Alan knew where the train station was, so they walked there. It took over an hour to get there. They arrived before the late train left for Springfield. Alan used three silver dollars from the lining of his coat to purchase their tickets.

Early the next morning they arrived in Springfield. They ate at the train station restaurant and had a fine breakfast. Alan then said, "We must look for some place to stay. If we can't find something in Springfield, we will continue south until we find someplace."

They headed south, walking. They passed a school at the south end of town. Just south of the school, was a small farm. They stared at it through the fence and it looked abandoned.

Betty Sue said, "That place looks like no one lives there. What do you think?"

Alan stared at it some more. The house stood back from the road, but was near the school. A chain link fence separated the school from the barn that was close to the fence. He noticed a windmill that wasn't turning and the wind was blowing, so he knew the windmill blades were shut off.

Alan said, "Let's walk around and come up the road like we're visiting. We'll knock on the door and ask for directions if someone is there."

They knocked, but no one answered. Alan tried the door, but it was locked.

He said, "Just look at the dust that has accumulated on the porch. No one has lived here in sometime. Let's try the backdoor."

They walked around, but the backdoor was locked also. The house set on a concrete foundation and you had to use steps to get up to the porch.

Alan saw an empty rain barrel and rolled it up to one of the windows. The screen over the window was locked. However, he had a pin knife, and was able to unlock the screen. He pulled it up and ducked under it, as he tried the window. It moved some, but was somewhat stuck. He knew then it wasn't locked, so he used all his might and the window slide up enough for him to squeeze into a bedroom.

"Go around to the backdoor and I'll let you in, Betty Sue."

She smiled at him and said, "You are so smart, Alan," then left and met him just as he opened the backdoor. They went through the house, and could tell no one had lived there in some time.

Alan said, "This is perfect. School starts next month, and we can enroll and live here. I have enough money to last us for awhile. I'll try to get work after school. I think we can make it."

Betty Sue came to him and hugged him tightly. She said, "It will be just like we are married, Alan. I'll clean the house and cook like mother did. I watched mother cook and remember some of it. I can cook pancakes and biscuits. I can also fry bacon and cook eggs. We will need chickens, and later on a cow. It's too late for a garden, but we can plant potatoes, onions and yams. Oh, I am so happy, Alan. I hope we can spend the rest of our lives here!"

"Well, don't get your hopes up, Betty Sue. Someone owns this place, and will come back sometime. It looks like it has been abandoned a long time. But someone owns it, and will come around, I'm sure. However, we need to scrub it down.

They investigated each room. Alan said, the sheets are clean in both the bedrooms, the comforters have been over the beds and kept the pillows and sheets clean. All we have to do is put the comforters on the clotheslines, and beat them until all the dust is gone."

One bedroom was completely empty. Alan said, "The people who used to live here must have wanted their bed. We don't need it anyway."

Betty Sue looked apprehensively at Alan and said, "You won't make me sleep all alone in my own room will you, Alan?"

Alan came over and hugged her and said, "No. Betty Sue. I said, I would never leave you, and that means at night, too."

She squeezed him tightly around the neck and said, "I love you Alan, I wish you would marry me."

Alan laughed and said, "You know we're too young for that, but just like I said, "I'll be your dad, mother and brother rolled up into one.

"Let's get busy now, we have a lot of cleaning to do."

Betty Sue went to work. She found a broom and started sweeping.

"It will be fun doing this, Alan. I've never been this happy. I just hope we can live here at least a year."

Alan said, "While you're sweeping, I need to go outside and inspect the barn." Alan found a hay loft that was filled with hay. It was in bales with wire holding it. It was brown on the outside like it had been there a long time, but he pulled some of the hay back and it was still green on the inside.

He found a bin that was nearly full of maize and a crib full of corn. The corn was hard, but Alan knew that animals could eat it.

He then went to the windmill. It had a wooden tank beside it. The tank was covered, but there was a hatch you could life up to look inside. Alan used a ladder that was there and looked into the tank. It was empty. He could then see there was a cable that kept the windmill blades from turning. He pulled the lever that locked the blades. The blades creaked, and slowly turned at first, then picked up speed. In just seconds, water began pouring into the tank. He saw that tank supplied water to the house's kitchen, sink and bathroom. There was also water to the barn and a faucet in the garden area, so it could be irrigated.

Alan returned to the house and Betty Sue said, "The water is running in the bathroom."

Alan went in and saw that the tub faucet had been left open so that it drained the pipes in the house to keep them from freezing in the winter. He turned the faucet off and then leaned down and turned the valve to the toilet and the tank started filling.

He grinned at Betty Sue and said, "All the comforts of home."

The kitchen had a kerosene stove. On the back porch was a barrel that was half full of kerosene. Alan filled the stoves tank and lit the stove. It worked perfectly. They opened the cupboards and there were plates, glasses, cups and saucers and the usual things that were used to eat. They looked in the drawers and there was silverware.

Betty Sue found pots and pans in the draws and said, "They were nice enough to leave their cooking ware."

What had happened was, Mr. Vetter, the man who sold the farm, wanted to buy all new cooking and eating ware, as those that they had were twenty years old, and he wanted to give his wife all new ware for their new kitchen.

Alan and Betty Sue placed all the eating ware on the table and washed the cupboards and drawers as they had accumulated dust for the last year. There was also a pantry that they cleaned thoroughly. They spent the rest of the day cleaning.

Alan said, "We will need some food for tonight and tomorrow. I saw a store across from the school. We'll go there and stock up some."

Betty Sue said, "There's a small wagon next to the house that we can use to pull our groceries home."

At the store the owner said, "Are you new in this area?"

Alan said, "Yes, my folks just rented the place behind the school."

"Oh, the Vetter's place. I heard he sold out, and moved right downtown. He was smart to go before he was too old to move. I'll miss them. They were nice people. However, we have you to replace them."

Alan bought all the staples that they would need, plus a dozen eggs, a pound of bacon, flour, potatoes, onions and all the necessary thing. He also bought bread and a salami.

The grocer said, The McCarthy's live across the highway from you. I'll bet he'll furnish you with many vegetables from his garden as everything is turning ripe. He always raises twice to three times what they need, even after canning."

Alan said, "Thanks, Mister. We'll do that. I bet if I rake up his barnyard he'll pay me in vegetables."

It was now after five and they hadn't eaten since their breakfast, so they were both starved. Betty Sue was good to her word. She made pancakes, scrambled eggs and bacon. She cooked a good dinner for them, while Alan set the table.

The next day Alan went across the highway and introduced himself. He told Mr. McCarthy that his dad had rented the Vetter's place. He asked if he could rake his barnyard and keep his chicken coop clean, in exchange for four hens and a rooster.

McCarthy said, "Sounds like a good exchange. I like exchanges rather that paying for something. It makes better sense."

Alan carried the chickens home in gunny sacks. He then went to the chicken pen. There were nests there that he rejuvenated, and the hens began laying eggs. They didn't eat the eggs as they wanted more chickens.

They went across the street and raked the barnyard once a week and cleaned his chicken pen. They always loaded their wagon with every kind of vegetable you could name.

Alan said, "My father is out of town and mother passed away some time ago."

Using the McCarthy's plants, they planted potatoes, beets, carrots, radishes and other vegetables that grew under the ground. They kept busy doing things around the house and barn.

Their hens now had baby chicks and now all they needed was a cow. They knew they would have to wait on that. They even talked McCarthy into giving them a nanny and billy goat as he had a lot of goats. Alan said, "Anytime you need me, I will work for you and charge you nothing."

McCarthy said, "You're a good neighbor, Alan, you can call on me the same."

After Alan was home he said, "A cow may be too much for us. I like goat milk and as our herd builds, we will slaughter one of them for meat."

"Do you know how to do that, Alan?"

"No, but I'll ask Mr. McCarthy how. He'll probably come over and help me the first time."

Everything went great and in September they went to school. Alan explained that their mother was deceased and their father had to leave town for a few days because of his job. They gave the name of Alan and Betty Sue Reclin. Alan had his birth certificate, and told the principal that they had lost Betty Sue's. He accepted that, and soon they were enrolled in school.

When it turned cold, they closed all the doors to the kitchen and just stayed there until bedtime, as it was the only place they could heat. It was a cold winter, but both had wool coats and caps. Betty Sue insisted that Alan sleep with her to keep her warm, of course.

CHAPTER 2

Kyle Allen

Kyle Allen had graduated from high school and was looking for a job. He wanted to go to college, but his mother and father had been ill, and didn't have the money to help him. He had an Uncle Paul, who was a printer for the Chicago Tribune. He had a modest income until a friend of his, put him onto a night job.

He found out that the job was printing forged twenty dollar bills for a mobster named Dion O'Banion. O'Banion had been a waiter and singer at McGovern's saloon and cabaret. There, he met a small time gangster named, Gene Gary. They became friends and it wasn't long until they formed a gang, with Dion their leader. They did small jobs until they met a forger who told them about the plates of a twenty dollar bill he was working on. He said, "I don't have the money to print the bills, but I see you do. If you'll back me, we can make a ton of money. These plates are good. I've worked five years on them. In Philadelphia I can buy the proper paper and ink necessary to print twenty dollar bills that can pass anywhere. If you will furnish the money, I'll go there and buy them."

Dion furnished the money and sent him to Philadelphia to purchase what he needed.

By this time, the O'Banion's gang was bootlegging whiskey from Canada and making a sizable profit by doing so. He expanded his business, and now owned several speakeasies that were doing a landslide business. His liquor was the best, and he had some real talent in his shows. He had managers who were good at what they did. Money began flowing in at an incredible rate.

The internal revenue service was on everyone's case, now, if they suspected they were doing illegal business. Dion decided to just deposit in the banks what most business did. That way, it would look like he was legit to the feds. He stored the rest of the cash money in cardboard boxes.

Dion purchased a three storied building with a basement. He needed to renovate the building as it was old. He set up his office on the first floor. He had an office that was quite large. He decided to wall off a back portion of his office and create a storeroom behind it. The store room had no windows or doors except the one to his office.

It was a great place to store all the money he had in cardboard boxes. He had a great security system with a man at the front door and one just outside his office.

The heating system was from floor furnaces that were not only expensive to run, but couldn't heat the building properly in the dead of winter. He decided to put in steam heat to adequately warm the building. Doing this was quite pricey, but he was able to blackmail a heating contractor, so the job was done at cost. The steam heaters had a boiler room in the basement that was just below his office and storeroom. The system needed tending from five in the morning until five in the evening

Kyle's uncle Paul had now been hired to print the bogus twenty dollar notes and the presses were set up at the far end of the basement of the building that Dion had purchased. Dion was talking to Paul one day when the workmen were constructing the new steam heaters. He told Paul that he needed someone to tend the boilers from five in the morning until five in the evening. Paul said, "I have a nephew who needs a job."

Dion said, "Is he trustworthy?"

"Sure," He comes from a good family. He wanted to go to college, but his dad took sick and he needs the job. I'll vouch for him."

Dion said, "Bring him with you tomorrow. I like to hire people that I know. Family is good. I will have the workmen show him what has to be done."

Paul brought Kyle the next day, and took him to the basement to learn what he had to do. It was an easy job. It required Kyle to come in at five in the morning, and get the boilers going, then add the proper water. During the day he just had to monitor the water and pressure, and add the amount of coal needed to keep the boilers going. He liked the job and it gave him a lot of free time.

Kyle liked to read, but all he had was kerosene lamps, and his end of the basement had no windows. The building had been wired for electricity during the renovation, but only the end where Kyle's uncle worked had electricity. Kyle knew if he could somehow bring some wiring to the basement from the room upstairs, he could have adequate light. He had worked with his dad when electricity came available for houses in Chicago. They wired their entire house and Kyle knew the principles of electrical wiring after that. He thought about bringing electricity from where his uncle worked, but there was no way to hide the wiring. He then thought of bringing some insulated wires and running them in a conduit from the basement up to the room above, he could connect the wires and have an electric light to read by. That would be simple.

He was pretty sure that Dion would not approve of him bringing wiring from his office so he began to think how he could covertly do the wiring.

He examined the ceiling and discovered where the old floor furnace had been. There was a grate that had been used by the floor furnace that had been closed up. Early one morning before anyone arrived at the building, Kyle started working on the boards that closed up the grate. He had to work quietly as there was a guard outside Dion's office. He removed one board then the others came easily. After removing the boards, he found he could remove the grate just by pushing it up.

He climbed into the room and found it was a storeroom. A string to an overhead light was there so he turned on the light that hung from above. He looked for electrical outlets on the wall and found one near the grate. He had to move some boxes to do that and one of them popped open. He stood and stared at the contents of the box, it was full of cash. The box containing all denominations of cash notes except ones. He noted twelve boxes that he was sure contained cash, also. The boxes had dust on them, so he knew they were just being stored there. He estimated that there must be a million dollars or more in cash. He was utterly amazed. He resealed the box that was open and then looked at the electrical outlet on the wall. He could see where he could put in his conduit down the inside of the wall by simply pushing it up from the basement. He then inserted his wires into the conduit, connect the wires to the electrical outlet and he was in business. No one would be the wiser after he put the cover for the plug back in place.

He jumped down to the basement then put the grate back in place. He put the boards back loosely that covered the grate. He sat and thought about all that cash.

That very week his folks passed away. While Alan was at work the vent to the gas heater in his folks' room somehow was turned shut. When Alan returned home he found both were dead. It was a terrible time for Alan.

His Uncle Paul did all the arrangements. They stood together at a graveside funeral. His Uncle Paul said, "We now only have each other."

Alan always had lunch with his uncle Paul at a café that was close to their building. His uncle Paul said, "They're shutting down my part of the operation. They told me they had more than enough bogus money now. They don't know it, but I printed out all the paper and most of the ink to stay ahead of them. I have over a hundred thousand dollars worth of twenties. I would like to store them someplace, so they don't know I did this. It would be a shame to just burn the money. Do you have some place to hide two boxes?"

"Sure, Uncle Paul. I have a place behind the boiler that no one knows about. I can put the money there."

So after lunch they returned, and both carried a box to the boiler room. Kyle had an old tarp to put over the boxes, then stacked some old boards from the construction on the tarp.

They sat and talked then. His uncle said, "You know, Dion doesn't like loose ends, and I'm a loose end. I think it would be better for my health if I pull out of here. I'll write you when I'm established somewhere else. Get a post office box under an assumed name and write me a letter in Philadelphia, general delivery, under the name of Lester Drake. Can you remember that?"

Kyle said, yes, I will use the name, Paul Drake. How long will it take you to get there?"

"I'm leaving tonight. I should be there next week." Paul left and Kyle began to think. *If I were to use that bogus money and replace the bottom half of each box with the cash upstairs, I would be rich. Of course, I would have to cover my trail so they could never find me.*

He transferred the bogus bills and put them in the bottom of the boxes of the cash upstairs. As the boxes had dust on them, Kyle thought it may be years before anyone knew about the bogus bills. He opened each of the twelve boxes upstairs and placed the bogus bills on the bottom of each of them. He then put the bills he took, into the two boxes that had contained the bogus bills. When he had the cash in the basement, he carefully put the boards back like they were under the grate.

There was a door to the alley from the back of the basement that no one used. He found his key to the building also fit the alley door. Kyle oiled the old lock then used his key and it opened easily. He came at night with a suitcase and carried the cash home. It took two trips. He then counted it. It came to a little over two hundred thousand dollars. At five each morning he opened the building. Only the inside guard was on duty. Kyle had a thermos and always gave a cup of coffee to the guard, who sat at a desk just outside O'Banion's office.

Kyle had a friend, Tim Clark, who went to his church. He was the same age as Kyle. Unfortunately his friend had tuberculosis (T. B.) and now just stayed at home with his parents. Kyle went to see him quite often as he felt sorry for him. Tim's folks told Kyle of a sanitarium near Pueblo, Colorado that treated T. B., and had been successful with some patients.

Mr. Clark said, "I wish we could send him there, but we don't have the money."

Kyle went to his doctor, which was Tim's doctor also, and had him check him for T. B. The doctor said, "The patch test shows you have been exposed, but that doesn't mean you'll ever come down with it. I will have to report you to the state as it is now a law that I do so."

Kyle was thinking, "If I could get Tim to Colorado and switch birth certificates with him I would have a cover. He then wrote the sanitarium in Pueblo to obtain the cost, and what was needed to enter the sanitarium. The return mail said it would cost $30 dollars a month, and he must have his birth certificate. Kyle then told the Clarks that he would furnish the money for Tim's treatment in Colorado.

He said, "I was saving for college, but I can see that will never happen, so what better way to spend it than to save Tim's life."

Mr. Clark was a proud man and surely didn't want to take money from Kyle, but he loved his son and didn't want him to die, so he accepted Kyle's offer. Mr. Clark was retired and decided to move he and his wife to Colorado to be near their son.

Kyle said, "I want to go with you to see if it is a place Tim will like." The Clarks were more than grateful.

Kyle gave a two weeks notice. He told O'Banion that he had contacted T. B. and would be going to Colorado to a sanitarium for treatment. O'Banion was a hypochondriac and after Kyle left, he had all the door knobs wiped down with a disinfectant. Kyle now had time to hide the money. He had decided on using the metal lockers at the bus station.

Kyle instructed the man who was taking his place, before he left. As he was leaving, Dion asked, "What happened to your uncle, Kyle?"

"He told me he was going to California. He said he would write me when he got settled, but never has."

Dion said, "I would surely like to know where he is in case I need him again."

Kyle thought, *"I bet. You mean so you can bump him off."*

The move to Pueblo was not to be for a couple of months as Mr. Clark needed to sell his house. During that time, Kyle took a train south to Springfield. He wanted to relocate away from Chicago. He found a land agent named Bob Moore. Kyle told him he was interested in buying a place. He wanted it on the edge of town with a few acres, incase he wanted to grow some feed. He said he might want to run a few head of cattle, later. The land agent said, "How much do you have to spend?"

"I have enough money to buy any place I want, but I want a bargain."

"Just like everyone," Bob replied. He then said, "I have a friend who mentioned that he may want to sell out. The place is south of town, next to the new school that was built. As a matter of fact, my friend, Carl Vetters, sold half of his property to the school district. Your house sets very near the school. Do you have any children?"

"Not at this time," so Bob didn't ask further questions, as he thought maybe this was private business. Bob then said, "I didn't get your name."

Kyle said, "Paul Drake. Let's go see the property."

Bob had a car and they drove to the place that was on the main road south. They turned into a driveway that took them to a house. They were met by a man in his seventies. Bob introduced him as Carl Vetters. Carl invited them in, and they discussed the price of the house."

Carl said, "Effie and me thought it would take a year or so to sell this place. I sold half of it two years ago to the school district. That's why our barn sits just twenty feet from the back of the school. They built a strong chain-link fence between us, so you won't have any kids wandering over. All the school's facilities are on the other side of the school, anyway.

"I have a good windmill and a tank high enough to furnish the barn and house with water. The pipes above the ground are insulated and we have had no trouble with them freezing on us. I have enough hay to last a winter for your cows and a lot of corn and maize for your other animals."

Kyle said, "I will not be moving for sometime, so you can sell your animals and chickens. I may be a year or two before

I will occupy the house. I just wanted a place to keep some of my things, as I wanted out of the city. My uncle left me a considerable amount of money when he died. I was amazed as it was all in cash. He never trusted banks."

Bob said, "Cash is great."

They finally settled on three-thousand, two-hundred dollars for the place. Carl said, "I have been inquiring about a place downtown that is near a grocery store and the post office. When you return to sign the papers next week, we may be moved."

Kyle said, "That will be okay with me."

A week later Kyle had his place. Carl and Effie had left most of the furniture, but one bedroom of furniture that they took with them. Carl said, "I want to give Effie all new furniture for our apartment, but we like our bed." They also left their dishes and pots and pans as they could tell Paul Drake was a bachelor, and probably didn't have any of those things. Carl told Effie he wanted her to have all new dishes and pots and pans as theirs were twenty years old.

Kyle was fixed now. He was out at his new place alone. He looked for a place to hide most of his newly gained fortune. He didn't want to deposit it, as that may draw suspicion. He decided to invest a quarter of his money into the stock of the Chicago Water and Power Company through a local broker who he had told the story of the cash his uncle had left him. He invested another quarter of his money in a New York utility company. He knew people would always need utilities and this was the safest place he knew. Both also paid a healthy dividend. He did deposit nine-hundred and twenty dollars in the local bank under the name of Paul Drake to match the deed of his property. He would also have the Utility companies pay the dividends directly into his bank account in Springfield.

Half of his money needed to be hidden, but where? He noticed a concrete pig trough that sat away from all structures. He decided to dig out from under the trough and place a six-inch threaded wrought iron pipe, ten feet long and place it under the edge of the trough. The pipe could contain all his money and be sealed on each end with pipe caps. He then covered the pipe and made it look like the other ground around it. Fire or water could not destroy his money. The pigpen had not been used in several years and would not be used while he owned the property.

Kyle bought two thirty-six inch pipe wrenches to open and close the pipe caps. The pipe wrenches he kept in the barn in a tool box. He then felt he was safe.

A month later he was on a train for Pueblo, Colorado with Tim and his parents. Kyle had not told Tim and his parents that Tim needed his birth certificate.

When they arrived in Pueblo, Kyle said, "I'll go out to the sanitarium and see if we have everything they require to enroll Tim. I will also pay them for the first six months."

When Kyle returned he said, "Do you have Tim's birth certificate? He will need that." Kyle knew they didn't.

Tim's father said, "No, we never picked that up from the courthouse."

Kyle said, "I have mine. Just register him under my name. No one will know the difference."

They all agreed that this was the only thing they could do, as who would know the difference? So Tim was now registered under the name of Kyle Allen.

Kyle stayed a week, as he could see Tim was very ill now, and thought he may never see him again. As Kyle rode the train back, he decided to go to Philadelphia and look up his uncle Paul. He wanted to warn him that Dion was looking for him.

Arriving in Philadelphia he went to one of the newspapers there and looked for a printer under the name of Lester Drake. He was in luck, the very newspaper he was at employed his uncle. They showed him where his uncle was working.

His uncle Paul was astounded that Kyle had found him. Kyle said, "I knew you were coming to Philadelphia and you gave me the name of Lester Drake, so it was easy. Dion doesn't know the things I do. However, he asked where you were, so I thought I had better warn you. I told him you were in California, but he's pretty cagy and may not buy that.

"I'm now living in Springfield, Illinois under the name of Paul Drake. I have a post office box there, so you can write me. Let's make it a rule that after we receive a letter from one another, we will immediately burn it, so we could never be traced. I'm probably just being overly cautious. Dion probably doesn't want to kill you."

"Don't underestimate Dion. He is thorough, and he sees me as a liability. He won't spend a lot of money looking for me, but he will make sure, I'm not in the Chicago area. I think I'm safe here in Philadelphia under an assumed name.

"What are you going to do now, Kyle?"

"I don't know. I think I will just think about that for awhile. I might go to college."

"And become what?"

"I don't know that either, but I'll figure it out."

"Are you still working for Dion?"

"No, I have a friend who has T. B. Because I visited him a lot, I was exposed to the disease. The doctor had to report me to the health department, but told me that being exposed was probably good, as I was probably immured to it now. I told Dion, I had it and was going to Colorado to a sanitarium. You know what a hypochondriac Dion is. He won't go near me again. He probably had the basement fumigated," and they both laughed.

"You covered your tracks good, but if I were you I would stay away from Chicago. I'm going to New York as if Dion is looking for you, he will try to get me and pry the information out of me. I'll be looking around for a job. If you don't hear from me don't worry. I'll contact you in a year or so."

Kyle stayed just two days, then decided to go to New York City, as he always wanted to go there. He stayed there a week then decided to go to London and then on to see Paris. He took ten thousand dollars with him and thought, "When this runs out I'll return to my farm.

CHAPTER 3

Life On The Farm

Alan and Betty Sue were happy on the farm. However, Alan could see that they would need money. He had no idea how he could earn some. He decided that come spring he would try to make a deal with the McCarthy across the highway, and let him farm the six acres on the half-shares. That would bring in some cash in the fall.

However, in the back of his mind was the gnawing of the real owner showing up and kicking them out or worse, sending them to the reformatory.

At school one day, Betty Sue overheard Miss Duncan talking to the principal, Mr. Farley. Mr. Farley had taken a job in Chicago and Miss Duncan had a room with him and his wife.

Miss Duncan said, "What will I do? No one will rent a room to an unmarried woman. She was nearly in tears when Mr. Farley left.

Betty Sue, having an enterprising mind, went to Miss Duncan and said, "My dad travels a lot, but I'm sure he would rent you a room, Miss Duncan?"

A smile of gratitude crossed her face and she said, "When can I see him?"

"He's out of town for a few days, but Alan handles all the business for him. Alan and I discussed taking on a roomer with dad before he left. He asked us to look around for a nice person, and you certainly are that."

"Where do you live, Betty Sue?"

"That's the good part. It's just south, next door to the school"

"My, that is convenient. May I come over tonight?" asked Miss Duncan.

"Sure, why not. How about seven, tonight. It will be good to have you with us."

"Where is your mother?"

Betty Sue looked very sad and said, "The flu took her."

Miss Duncan said, "I'm so sorry. However, it looks like a good fit. I will see you tonight."

Betty Sue couldn't wait to tell Alan. He said, "Betty Sue, you are the smartest girl in the world. We will charge her ten dollars a month, and that will give us enough to eat on."

Miss Duncan was a nice looking woman with a shapely figure. She was twenty-two and had never been married. She was religious, and always went to church each Sunday.

She came promptly at seven. Alan showed her the bedroom she would occupy, then the kitchen.

Betty Sue said, "We want you to feel like this is your home, and we are your children. Tell us our chores, and we will mind you as if you were our mother."

Miss Duncan said, "I love it here, how much must I pay?"

Alan said, "Is ten dollars a month too much?"

"Of course not. I will also contribute to the groceries. It looks like we are a family."

Miss Duncan moved in. After she was there just one day she said, "You father's room has no bed or furniture in it. Where will he sleep when he returns?"

Alan said, "He was sleeping in your room, and said he would buy a new bedroom set if we were to rent his room."

This satisfied Miss Duncan for the time being. However, the next day they were eating dinner and she asked, "Do you sleep with Betty Sue, Alan?"

"Yes, she's afraid of the dark, and it helps her if I'm close."

"Well, you are getting too big to sleep together. I think you should sleep in your dad's room on a pallet until your dad returns, then he will figure something out, like twin beds or something."

Betty Sue said, "Please, Miss Duncan, I have horrible nightmares, and if Alan is not there I can't stand it."

"Well, okay, but when your father returns, I will discuss this with him."

Everything went smoothly for a few weeks, and they became a family. However, one night at the dinner table, Miss Duncan looked at Alan and said, "There isn't a father, is there Alan?"

Alan was quiet for a moment and then said, "No ma'am. We just made that up. We're orphans just trying to make our way."

"Then how did you get this house?"

"It just stood vacant, so we moved in. No one has bothered us for nearly a year now, so we just continued to live here."

"There must be an owner. Why don't you or Betty Sue ask the fellow you rake up for. He will know who used to live here."

"That's a good idea, Miss Duncan. We'll do that tomorrow." Alan knew he must phrase his question just right, so when he asked, he said, "Were you friends with the people who used to live where we do?"

"Sure. Carl and Effie Vetters. They moved to town because they were getting to the point that the farm was too much for them. They live in an apartment house close to the post office. Just ask anyone downtown. Everyone knows Carl and Effie."

When they returned home, they reported what they had found out. Miss Duncan said, "Now you need to find the Vetters and ask them who they sold to."

The next day Betty Sue and Alan walked into town and went into the post office. They asked the clerk about the Vetters. The clerk said, "You're in luck, that's Carl coming in the door now." They turned and Carl smiled at them.

The clerk said, "These youngsters want to meet you, Carl."

Carl smiled and said, "I would like to know you, too. My name is Carl Vetters."

Alan said, "I'm Alan and this is Betty Sue. We now live at your farm and just wanted to meet you."

"You must be Paul Drake's children."

"Yes, we are, but daddy is a salesman, and is out of town most of the time. Betty Sue and I hold down the fort. We love the place, and we can see you loved it too, as everything is so neat, tidy and well built. We just wanted to know you, as we could see the love you had for that place."

"That is true. Why don't you come up and meet Effie. She will want to meet you. We don't get to see youngsters anymore. Our two sons were killed in the war, so we have no grandchildren. He smiled and said, "Maybe we can adopt you as grandchildren."

They went and met Effie. She fed them some muffins she had just baked. The Vetters had an instant like for the children, and made them promise to visit them each time they came to town. The children promised, and were off to the farm.

When they returned, Alan said, "Paul Drake owns this farm. We met the former owners and they live in town. They are really nice people, and just assumed we were Paul Drake's children. We didn't correct them, and just let them assume we were. I told them that our daddy was a salesman, and out of town much of the time."

"That will do for now, but there is going to be a time when he returns. Then what will we do?"

"Deal with it when he comes. He's probably a good guy and will give us time to make other arrangements."

"What arrangements? None of us have any money. You will probably be put in an orphanage and I will have to find someplace. Well, we will worry about that when the time comes. Meanwhile, try to think of something, you two. You're bright, or you wouldn't have gotten this far. By the way how did you get here?"

Alan looked at Betty Sue and she said, "Go ahead and tell her, Alan. She's like our mother now, so we had best bare our hearts to her."

Alan then told Miss Duncan everything, but the part that Betty Sue was not really his sister. Miss Duncan thought awhile and said, "I've never seen a brother and sister who loved each other as you two do. It's infectious and I love you two as if you were my children."

"You are our mother now, Miss Duncan," Betty Sue said.

Her sincerity was so poignant that Miss Duncan cried and pulled the children to her. She said, "I don't know how, but we'll always face life together. We are a family now, and you are my children.

"As much as I love you, you must always call me Miss Duncan at the school or our relationship would come up, and they would probably send you to an orphanage."

Life just continued on through the winter. Only one thing changed. They had all made friends with the janitor of the school, Hollis Henry. They told him how difficult it was to trudge clear out to the main road through the snow. If there were a gate between the school and their farm, they could be at school in seconds and go home for lunch.

Hollis knew a friend who had a chain-link gate. He told him the circumstances and the friend gave him the gate. He installed it, and they had him over for lunch. They now could eat lunch at home.

Their love grew and now Miss Duncan tucked them in each night and prayed with them. They prayed for the man who owned the property and for his safety. They asked that he be given a warm heart when he met them. Silently, Miss Duncan prayed that he would be a handsome man, who liked her. She had no boyfriends, but the children filled her life with joy, so that wasn't a hardship.

They all did things to improve the farm. Miss Duncan bought some discounted cloth and made curtains for the windows. Betty Sue swept the house each day and dusted it. Alan kept the barn clean. They also kept the yard free from weeds. They planted flowers in the spring and the place looked great from the road.

They had been there two years now and it was October of 1929. The stock market plunged, but nothing much changed with them. They knew men were out of work, but those that lived on farms, that were paid for, didn't feel any change.

CHAPTER 4

A Family And Tragedy

Kyle Allen reached London and loved it. He took an apartment in the Soho district and went to many dramas and shows. He met a young lady named Brenda. She was just his age. She lived not far from where he lived in an apartment with her folks. They were both fond of each other. Brenda invited Allen to meet her folks after a few months.

Her father was quite inquisitive. He asked, "What do you do for a living, Kyle?"

Kyle said, "My uncle left me a fortune, and I decided to see London then maybe Europe before I went back to America to settle down. I will go to college then. I think traveling has helped educate me. I own a small farm in America, so I have a home base. My parents passed away and I have no brothers or sisters, so I'm pretty much on my own."

This did not satisfy Brenda's father in the least. He thought maybe Kyle was a gangster of some kind. People didn't receive money just like that. He said he had no living relatives, so there was no way to check on him.

Her folks talked it over and thought they would send Brenda away to a woman's college. They knew one that was very strict, and kept the women away from men. They could only visit men from a nearby men's school that they were affiliated with. Brenda didn't like it, but there was nothing she could do.

Kyle followed her to the school, but after arriving, he saw he could not see Brenda. He wasn't in love with her, but thought he could be. He then thought, *"Well, I can't do anything about this, so I shall leave for Paris."*

In Paris, he saw immediately that he must learn the language. He enrolled in a language class and studied diligently. He went to the entertainment that was available and soon met several men his age. They introduced him to some of the women. The French had a much different culture than the English or Americans. He dated several of the women, and had a nice time, but knew he would never marry a French woman as they thought much differently than what he was used to. He stayed in Paris over a year and decided to visit Italy. He had seen some of the operas that the Italians performed and decided to visit their country.

He went to Rome, but it was too large, and he didn't speak Italian, so he decided he would not take the time, as he had in Paris, to learn the language. He went on to Naples and then on to the island of Capri.

He stayed there for a few weeks as most of the people there spoke English, as they dealt with many tourist from America and England. The people there were friendly, but their culture was much different. He became bored during the day, but the night life was good. He met a girl he liked, but then found she had another boyfriend.

He had now been gone for two years and his money was running out, so he decided to return to America. When he reached New York, everyone was in a panic as the stock market had crashed and many of the banks had closed.

Kyle was then glad he had most of his money in a pipe, rather than in a bank.

He caught a train from New York City, and was now in Springfield. He still had over a thousand dollars, so he decided to buy a car. He went to a dealer and purchased a model "A" Ford. The dealer showed him how to operate it and it wasn't long until he got the hang of it.

He drove out to his house, and could see that someone was occupying it. He decided to pose as a visitor looking to visit the Vetters. He drove up, and a woman and two children came out. Kyle got out of his car and with a smile on his face said, "I'm looking for the Vetters."

Alan said, "They moved into town a couple of years ago."

Kyle then looked at the woman and said, "Who might you be?" Still keeping the smile on his face.

Miss Duncan returned his smile and said, "I'm Miss Duncan."

"Do you own this place Miss Duncan?"

She said, "No, I rent a room here."

"May I ask who you rent from?" Here, she began to suspect that there was more to his question than it implied, so she said, "Won't you come inside, and have some cool water so we may talk this out?"

They all went inside and Kyle looked at Alan and said, "Is your father around?" He could tell Alan was very uncomfortable with the question.

Alan said, "My father is a traveling salesman, and is not here very often."

"What is his name?"

Miss Duncan could see that this man knew they did not belong here and said, "Who are you, Sir and why are you questioning us?"

Kyle decided to just lay his cards on the table. He said, "I'm Paul Drake, the owner of this property. I don't want to scare you, because I'm not a vindictive man. I just wanted to know how you came to live here."

Miss Duncan said, "The children came first. Their folks died, and they were put in an orphanage. The authorities were going to separate them, so they left the orphanage and came to Springfield. They were going to leave Springfield when they saw your house. It was unoccupied, so they decided to live here until the owner showed up.

"I on the other hand, was looking for a room to rent, when Betty Sue offered me a room here. I teach at the school next door, and could see it was very handy to the school. I didn't know at first that they were all alone, but after a month or so we all told our stories. As no one showed up to claim the property, we decided to stay until that happened. Now that time has come, so what are you going to do?"

"After hearing your stories, I am going to do nothing, but move in. I like a family and it seems I have one already here. This may sound absurd to you, Miss Duncan, but I suggest we marry. It will be a marriage of convenience as it will be in name only. If you were to stay here unmarried, I'm sure you would lose your job sooner or later. Just seeing how you love the children, and could not care for them without a house, I think you will see the logic of our marriage. The kids could claim me as their father, and all would be fine again. What do you say, Miss Duncan?"

"I have no family other than Alan and Betty Sue, so I accept your proposal, Mr. Drake. I have already forgotten your given name?"

"I'm Paul Drake. I suggest we go and get a marriage license and get married tomorrow. I know the Vetters, and will ask them to be our witnesses. We can say we have known each other for sometime, and decided to marry. We can act like we are in love. I will have the children's names changed to Drake, and we will just be one happy family. You will find me congenial, and never demanding. You and the children will have a good home, and I will have a family, which I always wanted. By the way, what is your full name, Miss Duncan?"

She smiled and said, "Yes, you should know that before we are married. I'm Sandra Ann Duncan, soon to be Sandra Ann Drake.

As there was no bed for Paul, he slept with Alan the first night and Betty Sue slept with Miss Duncan. The next day they went to town. First they took out a marriage license, then went by the Vetters to tell them the news. They went with them and talked the Vetter's minister into marrying them that day. At the ceremony Paul kissed Miss Duncan and she liked it.

They then went to a furniture store and bought a bedroom set that the dealer promised to deliver that day. Paul also bought a lot of sheets, blankets towels and other bathroom necessities that he had noticed were lacking.

He said, "Mrs. Drake, I want you to buy all the necessities that the house and you and the children need."

As they were driving back to the farm, Betty Sue said, "Can we now call you mom and dad?"

Paul said, "I would like that."

Sandra said, "I would like that, too, but at school, I'm Miss Dunca...... I mean Mrs. Drake. It will take the other students awhile to make the switch to Mrs. Drake. Just don't call me, mom."

As they were driving Paul said, "I'm not real wealthy, but I have enough cash to buy things we need, and I want you, Sandra, to start a list and get everything we need."

Sandra said, "I don't even know what you do for a living, Paul."

"I'm an investor. I live off the dividends of my stock and buy and trade stock. I'm not a genius at this, but make enough for us to live comfortably, plus I have a smart wife who has a teaching job."

"I thought everyone lost their money in the stock market."

"Most did, but I had my money in utilities and everyone has to have utilities, so my money was fairly safe.

"We will keep our money separate for awhile to see how this works out. I see us being a real family within a year."

To everyone's embarrassment, Betty Sue said, "You should start sleeping with dad tonight. I would if I were you, Mom."

"Betty Sue!" Sandra said.

"It's the truth. Sometimes I hug up to Alan when it's thundering or if I get cold. He keeps me so warm, and I love to be held by him."

Paul and Sandra could see that Betty Sue knew nothing about sex, so they just smiled at one another and Sandra said, "Well, if it thunders a lot, I might" and they all laughed.

It just took two months until Sandra was sleeping with Paul. They loved each other and the children were responsible for a lot of their love.

Kyle, now Paul, had found a stock broker and spent a lot of time there going over various stocks. The brokers name was David Merit. He began having coffee with Paul when no customers were in his shop, and they would talk stock.

Paul said, "I think this is the line of business I want to be in. How did you get educated to do what you do?"

"I got a degree from Purdue College in economics. It gave me a foundation, but I got most of my education getting a master's degree in business at Illinois. That said, most of everything I use in this business was on the job training. If you are serious about going into this business, I will give you pointers, but research is the backbone of trading. Just keep going through the data on a stock you think will do something, then take the plunge.

"How did you survive the bust, David?"

"I didn't have much money in the market. I collected coins and put a lot of my money in my coin collection. I'll show it to you sometimes, but don't tell anyone I have a collection. I have a safe, but I still don't want people knowing.

"Most people who were stock brokers quit the business. I saw an opportunity here in Springfield, and opened up shop. As you can see we still don't have a lot of clients."

Sandra was now invited to many social events and she brought Paul. The police chief took a liking to Paul as he was interested in the stock market, and they talked a lot about different stocks.

Alan didn't take up sports like a lot of his friends. This was mostly because he didn't want to leave Betty Sue alone. The two of them found things they both liked. Fishing was one of them. There was a lake not far from the school and they spent a lot of time there.

Betty Sue had a talent for drawing, and Sandra encouraged her by getting her into an art class at the high school. The teacher was reluctant to take her, until Sandra showed her some of Betty Sue's works. The teacher then said, "She needs to be here. I enjoy teaching children with talent, and Betty Sue has that."

As the high school was several blocks from Betty Sue's school, Paul would come by and take her in his car. He would then wait until the class was over, then drive her back. He enjoyed this time as it gave him time with Betty Sue. She liked it too, and they became close.

At home, while Betty Sue was busy painting or drawing, Alan discussed the stock market with Paul.

Paul said, "I'm going to send you to college, Alan, when you finish high school. I want you to be educated." If you learn enough, someday we may open our own brokerage firm. We both love to study it, so why not let it make us rich?"

Alan laughed and said, "We will always have Mom and Betty Sue to fall back on when we go broke," and Paul laughed.

Paul said to Sandra one night, "Don't you want children? I notice we never have sex when you are fertile."

"No. Right now, Betty Sue and Alan take all my spare time. I don't want to take away from that."

"We do love them, but nothing like they love each other. We finally broke them from sleeping together."

"Yes, but only twin beds. I know she goes to Alan's bed half the time. She's getting near puberty now. I have read where boys at Alan's age are at their sexual peak and the way Betty Sue loves him, I'm afraid of what could happen."

Paul said, "Alan loves her too much for him to do that. He would go without a woman all his life before he would harm Betty Sue."

"Yes, I think you're right, however it's time for me to tell her about sex. I hate to bring it up, but I'm a mom, and that's my duty. I'll have to think of the best way to approach the subject."

"I'm glad it's you and not me."

"Well, you ought to talk with Alan about it."

Paul said "I did and do you know what he said?"

"Tell me," Sandra said with large eyes."

"I said, Alan, we should have a talk about sex. He said, "Sure dad, what do you want to know," and we laughed 'till we cried.

When they had calmed down Sandra said, "Have you noticed that they have very few friends?"

"That's because they spend all their spare time together unless one of us is with them."

"When Alan's not with Betty Sue, he's with you talking stocks. You two like to be together. I'm glad you have that common interest."

Alan got up early one morning as he had heard a noise. It was barely light. He saw Paul in the pigpen with a heavy pipe wrench working on something under the concrete trough. He didn't say anything to anyone about Paul being there, but one day Paul was driving Sandra and Betty Sue to an art exhibit and Alan said, "I've seen all that art. I think I'll stay home and read."

When they left, Alan went out to the concrete trough and could tell one end had fresh dirt put over something. Alan got the shovel and discovered the pipe. He unearthed the pipe, then got the wrench, and took off the cap. The pipe was stuffed with cash. Alan thought a minute. He thought, *"If ever something came up, where Betty Sue and I had to leave, we would need money. There is so much money here, no one would miss a thousand. I will find a place to stash a thousand dollars. If we never need it, so be it, but it's our insurance."* He took the thousand and put it in a glass mason jar and buried it by the corner of the barn. He then put the cap back on the pipe and put the dirt back exactly as he had found it.

Alan went back inside to read his book, but he couldn't help thinking about all that money. He thought, *"How did Paul get all that money in cash. No one deals in cash except gangsters.* He was shocked when the word "gangster" came to his mind. Had Paul taken that money? How else could he have accumulated all that money in cash. He knew he wouldn't ask him, but the thought was there.

When the family returned Alan acted as natural as he could, but his life had changed some. Paul might not be the man he said he was. There was something mysterious about him. You would never know it, as he was just a loving, happy man, but there was something sinister in his background that was a mystery that may come out later.

Life was pleasant. Sandra was happy and in love with Paul. However, she even wondered about Paul. He told her that an uncle had left him a lot of money, but he never talked about that uncle and Sandra decided not to ever ask.

Paul did more investing, but never bought a stock that didn't pay a dividend. His utility stocks paid him enough so his family had everything they wanted.

Paul decided to take them on a vacation. None of them had ever been far except Paul, and he never talked about being in New York, Paris or Italy. He knew Sandra was smart enough to know it took a lot of money to travel like that.

He came up with the idea of going to the mountains in Colorado. They were all deliriously happy about the trip. They took the train to Denver then on down to Colorado Springs. The went to the top of Pikes Pike on the cog train. They then went to Boulder and hiked many trails in the mountains. They returned to Denver and explored the city thoroughly. They all loved Denver.

The family was at a lake when the sun was setting. Paul and Sandra were back some on a bench, and Alan and Betty Sue were at the edge of the water looking at a spectacular sunset. Betty Sue had her arm around Alan and he had his arm around her. They watched the two and then they turned to each other and hugged.

Sandra said, "They act like honeymooners."

Paul said, "Not even honeymooners love each other like those two."

"Neither will ever fall in love with someone else. They love each other too much. Is that healthy, Paul?"

"Healthy or not, I'm glad they love each other like that. It makes me love you more, just seeing them."

Sandra said, "At least they're not kissing each other."

Paul said, "Not yet."

Sandra said, "It's always been at the back of my mind that they are not related."

Paul said, "What? Why would you say a thing like that?"

"Number one, Betty Sue has never had a birth certificate and two, they look nothing alike. Three, I have never seen a bother and sister so close."

"Well, I will never investigate it. I love them too much. If we investigated, we may find out something we didn't want to know. Let's just enjoy them and let things come to whatever they will."

Sandra said, "They never give us any trouble like I hear other parents gripe about. We should just count our blessings and like you say, let things come to whatever they will. However, when Betty Sue reaches sixteen, don't' be surprised when she comes to us and tells us Alan is not her brother and she wants to be married."

"I don't think that is likely, but it could be."

They returned home as school was to start the next Monday.

CHAPTER 5

Trouble From Chicago

Back in Chicago, Dion had taken on two men, Max Crowley and Tom Grover. They had both been investigators for the Pinkerton Detective Agency. However, they had been caught shaking down a client, and were sent to prison for two years. They were now out and could not be employed by legitimate companies, so they turned to Dion. He liked them as they were smart and could discern bad deals and dealers. They were also without conscience and could kill and torture people as they thought it was fun.

It had been well over five years since Kyle had left the employment of Dion. Dion had just made a big payment to his liquor supplier in Canada in cash. A week later he was visited by the dealer. He handed Dion three bogus twenties and said, "Did you think I wouldn't find out?"

Dion looked at the twenties and said, "I swear, I didn't know the payments were made with these."

"It wasn't all bogus, but most of the twenties were. I wouldn't have noticed, but one of my bankers picked up on these. He said they were as good a forgery as he had ever seen, but they were bogus. He came to me instead of going to the cops as we help one another. I told him I would handle it."

"How much was bogus?"

"A little over twenty grand."

"I'll make it good in cash right now. I need to find out who swapped my cash and replaced it with phonies."

The first thing Dion did was to open the boxes of cash he still had on hand. He found over sixty-thousand dollars in bogus twenties. He had used several other boxes and no one had said anything about bogus twenties, so he didn't know how much had been swapped out.

He put Crowley and Grover on the case. They handled it just like they were on a job with the Pinkerton Agency. They first wanted to know when the bogus twenties were printed.

Dion said, "I had that scam going well over five years ago, but things were getting hot so I shut it down."

"Who did the printing for you?"

"A guy's named Paul Allen. I don't think he would make the swap, because we shut down his operation and cleaned out all the material that he was using and sold the press. He also knows that I would cause him much grief if he did such a thing."

"Regardless, we will investigate anyone who was around when the bogus bills were printed. Give me the names of all the people who were in the building since the bills were printed."

"That is all the people who works for me since I bought this building."

It was a short list and all but Paul and Kyle Allen were still working for Dion. The investigators went through the list quickly. All of them, but Paul and Kyle Allen lived modest lives and were quickly eliminated as suspects.

They asked Dion where Paul Allen was located. Dion said, "Funny thing, he just disappeared and I've not been able to locate him. He gave me the plates. I broken them in half, so no one could use them as evidence against me."

"What did you do with the broken plates?"

"I threw them in Lake Michigan."

One of the investigators looked at the other and said, "Paul Allen is our prime suspect."

"How could he get into the storeroom that houses the money?" Grover asked.

"He couldn't, I have a guard outside the door at all times."

"Allen could be in cahoots with one of your guards."

"I don't think so. The guards have been with me since I started. You've investigated them and they showed no spending. If they haven't spent any money for over five years, I don't think they are connected to the switch. There has to be another angle."

"Do you know where this Kyle Allen is? He was your boiler tender about the time the printing was done."

"Yeah, he got T. B. and went to an asylum in Colorado."

"We'll check the state's files, as all doctors have to report T. B. patients when they find them."

They went to the health departments and found Kyle had been reported. They also found the doctor's name and called on him. The doctor said, "Yes, he told me he was going to Pueblos, Colorado for treatment. He said he was coughing badly. I didn't think he had developed the disease, but with T. B., you never know."

They decided to write the sanitarium rather than make a trip. The sanitarium wrote back and said that Mr. Kyle Allen had passed away. They also sent a death certificate.

Crowley said, "Well, we're down to one suspect, now. We just have to locate him."

Grover said, "The kid could have stashed the money and never got to spend it."

"That is surely a possibility, but we need to eliminate the uncle before we draw that conclusion."

Grover said, "Let's find out where he lived before coming to Chicago. They found some of his friends and one of them knew Paul had grown up in Philadelphia.

Crowley said "We have a start." They were able to get a picture of Allen before they left for Philadelphia. With the photo, it was easy work to find Paul Allen.

They watched for him after work and he headed to a bar. He was at the bar and they got on each side of him. Grover said, "You don't spend much money for a rich man."

"What makes you think, I'm rich?"

"Because you have over a hundred-thousand of Dion O'Banion's money."

Paul was shocked. He said, "How do you know, Dion?"

"He sent us here to pick up his money. You can either give it up easily or later beg to give it up."

"Look, I wouldn't try to spend a cent of that bogas money. I like my freedom."

"We're not talking about bogus money. Dion is missing over a hundred-thousand dollars that you took from the boxes."

"What boxes, I don't know what you're talking about. I never took a cent from Dion. I'm not that crazy."

"Then who did? It's missing you know."

From just the expression on Paul's face, they believed him. Crowley said, "Then who could have taken it. Was it your nephew?

"I don't think so. He visited me about five years ago and would have said something if he had taken it."

"They told us he died of T. B."

"No, that must have been a friend of his. Kyle helped him get into a sanitarium in Colorado, then came and saw me. I hear from him about every two or three months."

"Where does he live now?"

"Springfield, Illinois. He has a post office box where I write."

"What name is he using?"

"Paul Drake."

"You better be telling us straight, because if you're not, it will be a very slow and painful death for you. We're artist at it and enjoy it."

They left, and a minute or two later, Paul left and wrote Kyle a letter about what had occurred and airmailed it.

Crowder said, "We don't really know this bird did it, but I'm sure the uncle didn't. The nephew was only nineteen when he worked for Dion. Do you think he was smart enough to pull that off and if he was, how did he do it?"

Grover said, "He was smart enough to cover his trail by giving his name to a dying person. That shows me a lot. Had the uncle not mentioned him, he would have gotten away with it."

They returned to Chicago, and went to the basement. They told the boiler tender to go have a drink at the bar, which he did. They started looking at the basement. The only electricity was from the light that was right under the storeroom. They noticed that the wires came down from the room up above where the boxes were. They had seen the basement and where the bogus money was printed.

Grover said, "I think the kid removed those boards to get a wire down here and discovered the boxes. No one could pass up an opportunity like that."

"How did he get the bogus twenties?"

"He probably stole them from his uncle."

They found how Kyle removed the boards and pushed up the furnace grate. They then caught the train to Springfield. They went to the post office and asked the clerk if he knew where Paul Drake lived. They were given the directions.

Paul and the family had just returned from Denver and Paul didn't get his mail. He thought he would get it Monday when the kids and Sandra were in school.

Paul, Sandra and the children returned on the Friday before school started. They were now getting ready for the school year. They would start the next Monday.

Paul had invested most of the money in the pipe now, and only had only about twenty thousand in the pipe. He kept that much for unforeseen emergencies.

Paul had told Sandra about having the cash stashed in the pipe and showed her where it was located. He did this so if anything happened to him she would not lose it.

It was Saturday and Paul was taking the kids to a movie. Sandra didn't want to go, as she had a to get some things ready for the school year that started Monday. They had been gone about a half hour when someone knocked at the door. She answered it and two men just shoved passed her with guns in their hands.

One said, "Are you alone?"

She was frightened and said, "Yes, my husband and children are out of town." Crowley said, "Are you the wife or girlfriend."

"The wife. We were married three years ago."

"Well, he must have told you about the money?"

"What money?" she asked.

"The money he stole from Dion O'Banion. Don't play dumb. It will go much easier on you if you just tell us where he keeps it."

"I really don't know what you're talking about. We have some cash, but not a lot. You are welcome to it, if you will just leave."

"Oh, we'll leave, but only if we have the hundred grand your husband has." With that said, Crowley slapped her very hard.

Sandra could see they meant business, so she said, "I'll take you to the money we have hidden." She led them to the barn to get the shovel and pipe wrenches. They then went to the pipe under the pig trough. They exposed it, and it only took them a moment or so to open the pipe. They took the twenty-thousand and went back to the house.

Grover said, "Where's the rest of it?"

"That's all there is. I'm being as honest as I can be. You've got to believe me."

With that Crowley said, "You know what we can do to you, you had better spill your guts, and with that, his hand went to the top of her dress and ripped it down past her waist."

Grover grabbed her bra and ripped it off. Crowley said, "You've got some nice tits there, sister. Now tell us where the rest of it is, as we can get much nastier."

She couldn't tell what she didn't know, so she decided to not say another word. They stripped her and both raped her. They then began to torture her by burning her arms with cigarettes. She screamed and screamed, but it did no good. They ended up cutting her throat and she bleed to death in seconds.

They left a note that read:

> Kyle Allen:
>
> This is just the beginning. We want the money you took from Dion.
>
> If Dion doesn't have the hundred-grand by next week. We are coming for your kids. They will be given worse treatment that your wife.

The note wasn't signed.

When Paul returned they were all devastated. Paul saw the note and put it in his pocket before the kids saw it.

They went to the police and the police told them to go to a hotel that night. Paul had noticed before he left that the pipe had been emptied of the cash. He told the police that he wanted to take the kids to a relative, and that he would be back the next day.

He drove them to Jacksonville, a town west of Springfield about twenty miles. He had met a friend of Sandra that was teaching there. She was married, but they had no children. Their house was just a block from the elementary school and the high school was just a block beyond that. Kyle thought the kids could enroll there while he tried to deal with this tragedy.

They arrived at Jacksonville just at dusk. They were invited in and Paul told of the tragedy. He asked Sandra's friend, Letty, if she could keep the children awhile. He said, "It's worth a thousand dollars to me. I don't know when I can return for them, but I will keep in touch."

Letty said, "You don't have to pay us, we would be glad to do it for you and Sandra."

"No, I know you and your husband have been saving to buy a house, and this will give you a chance to do that. I was left a very substantial legacy and it's something I would like to do."

Paul finally convinced them to take the kids. Alan and Betty Sue cried when he left and Letty could tell they loved him.

After Paul left, Alan began to think. He thought of the pipe that was filled with money. He thought, *"The men who killed mom are people who dad was mixed up with. They came for their money and all of it wasn't there, so they tortured and killed mom. They must be good to trace dad there. It took them five years, but they found him. Betty Sue and I are next. We need to get away, and get away fast. I need to get Betty Sue so far away, no one could find her. However, I need to get that money I hid at the farm before we go. Thank heavens I took that thousand or we would be dead meat. I don't think dad is thinking straight. If they traced him to Springfield with a new name, they can surely find us here in Jacksonville."*

Paul drove back to Springfield and instructed the mortuary where Sandra was taken, to just bury her. He paid the mortician, then said he would have a memorial and put up a stone at a later time. He explained that his family just couldn't deal with it now. He told the police chief to just lock up the house when they were through with it, and left him a key.

Paul said that he and the kids just wanted to get away from Springfield for awhile. The Chief of Police understood.

The chief said, "Keep in touch with me, Paul, I'll do everything in my power to solve this case. It looks like some bad guys just broke in and did this terrible thing to your wife. We'll do our best to catch them."

CHAPTER 6

The Escape

Alan thought he would wait until tomorrow to tell Betty Sue they were leaving Jacksonville. The next day Letty took them to their schools. Betty Sue would go to an elementary school just a block away and Alan would attend the high school where Letty taught just a block after that.

They went into the elementary school and Letty talked to the principal in his office. She told of what had happened to the children's mother. He had read it in the papers. He told Letty he would handle it, and just go on to her school with Alan.

Alan and Betty Sue sat patiently outside the principal's office while Letty was talking to him.

Alan said, "You've got to trust me, Betty Sue. Bad things will happen if we stay here. As soon as the principal takes you to your room and leaves, tell the teacher you have to use the bathroom. When you leave the room walk out the door at the end of the hall. It does not go by the principal's office. Walk straight back to Letty's house and wait for me. I'll be there shortly, if I'm not already there."

Alan told her with such sincerity that Betty Sue didn't ask questions. She just followed his instructions to the letter. Alan did the same thing as Betty Sue and left the high school They met at Letty's house. Alan left a note that said:

Letty,

We have to go. If we stayed, it would only cause you and us to be in danger.

Thank you for your hospitality. Give dad his note.

Alan

They then walked to the Greyhound bus station. Alan bought two tickets to Springfield. The bus would pass right by the farm and Alan knew that. He told the bus driver that he and his sister wanted off at their farm and the driver stopped.

Alan retrieved the money while Betty Sue put food in Alan's knapsack. He then thought about his birth certificate and some other identification papers that told of their name change to Drake. They were all in the tin box and he retrieved them. In the box was over two hundred dollars in cash. He took that, also. He thought that Paul may think the gangsters took it along with the papers.

They started walking to the train station. Alan thumbed, hoping to catch a ride, and they did. Mr. McCarthy, who lived across the highway from them, gave them a ride. He hadn't heard of the tragedy yet, and they didn't mention it. They just said they were going downtown.

He dropped them off at the train station as Alan pointed to the movie theater that was close. After he left, they went into the train station and bought tickets to Chicago.

Alan then had time to explain their situation to Betty Sue. He said, "The men who killed mom, will come back for us. They think dad stole money from them. So they are out to make life as miserable for dad as they can. That means killing us.

"Dad thought he was putting us someplace safe with Letty, but if they traced him to Springfield, it wouldn't take them long to find us. I need to get you to a safe place where no one can find us."

Betty Sue looked into Alan with her big brown eyes and said, "I trust you with all my heart."

Alan brought her to him and they stayed hugged for awhile. Their train number came up and they were off.

Betty Sue said, "Have you figured out where we're going?"

Alan grinned and said, "No, but I'm working on it."

"Just so we're together Alan. If we parted, I would die."

"We'll never part as long as I have breath in me."

In Chicago, Alan was looking at the board that told destinations. He saw San Francisco. He looked at Betty Sue and said, "How would you like to see San Francisco, Betty Sue?"

"Anywhere you are, is alright with me. They went to the window to buy their tickets. The clerk said, "Will you need a Pullman?"

"What's a Pullman?"

"It's a sleeping berth for nighttime."

"Yes, we'll take two."

"No, Betty Sue said, "Just one."

The clerk raised an eyebrow and Betty Sue said, "We're brother and sister."

The clerk said, "Well, it will surely save you money, but it may be a bit crowded."

They were in their seats and Alan said, "Mom was right, we're getting too old to be sleeping together."

Betty Sue said, "Then we should get married. I know all about sex, mom taught me. It doesn't embarrass me a bit talking sex with you, Alan. We can talk about anything.

"Well, sex or no sex, we are getting too old to sleep together, and we're too young to be married. If we tried to do that, they may send us back to the orphanage."

Alan knew Betty Sue would not want that, and that's why he said it.

They liked the train trip as they knew they were safe. Alan said, "We will surely miss dad and mom, but if we were with Paul, our lives wouldn't be worth a plugged nickel. I just know those people were after some money dad took from them. They caught mom alone and killed her to make daddy give them the money. However, with us gone, dad can handle them much better, not having us to worry about."

"How do you have the money for us to travel, Alan?"

"I discovered a large pipe that dad had hidden. It contained thousands of dollars. When I looked at all that cash, I thought of you. If we ever had to make a run for it again, we would need cash. So I took a thousand dollars. There was so much money I didn't think anyone would miss a thousand. I buried it in a glass jar and when we went back to the farm, I dug it up while you were packing food for us.

"With all that cash in the pipe, that's when I realized dad was into something illegal. No one has that kind of cash, but gangsters. I don't think dad's a gangster, but I think he took a large amount of money from them. That's why they'll be after us. They tried to get mom to tell them where the money was, but she didn't know, so they killed her.

"I know dad feels badly about that. That's why we have to get away from all that. Mom is dead and dad might as well be, because we can never see him again. But we have each other, Betty Sue, and that's all that matters."

She smiled at him and kept her large brown eyes on him. Alan said, "You're becoming good looking, Betty Sue."

"You just say that because you love me so much. I could be fat, cross-eyed and snaggled toothed, and you would think I was beautiful. That's what loves all about," and she came into Alan's arms and hugged him.

Alan said, "That may be true, but I have eyes and you're becoming beautiful."

"Yes, but I will be an old maid before you marry me."

"You're only thirteen, for Pete's sake."

They were in their sleeper and were putting on their night shirts. Being nude before each other didn't bother either of them.

When they were lying on their backs thinking, Betty Sue said, "Do you ever have an erection like mother told me men have?"

"My gosh, Betty Sue, you should never ask those kind of questions."

"Well you once told me that you would be my daddy, mother and brother all rolled up into one. I don't have mother anymore, so I need to have those questions answered."

Alan said, "Well okay. All men have erections, it's just part of life."

"When you get one, can I see it?"

Alan then laughed and said, "Betty Sue you are the limit. When we marry you can see it, but not until then."

"I can't wait that long, Alan, please show me, if one comcs up."

Alan just laughed.

They laid there a long time and Alan was about to go to sleep when Betty Sue said, "I sometimes get this wonder feeling between my legs. I rubbed it there and got the most wonderful feeling I ever had."

Alan said, "Well, please don't do it in front of me. Those things should be done in private."

"Do men rub themselves the same way girls do, sometimes?"

"Yes, men sometimes do. Now go to sleep before I give you a spanking."

"You've never given me a spanking. Other girls talked about their mothers spanking them when they were bad. I never got a spanking."

"There is a reason why you never got a spanking. You were always good, until tonight."

"Why don't you like to talk about sex, Alan. It's just another body function like going to the toilet. That's what mom said."

"Well, she's right in a way, but you don't talk about going to the bathroom, either. Now for Pete's sake go to sleep. He turned over facing the wall and Betty Sue turned over, also, and hugged up to his back.

In just a few minutes, Betty Sue was breathing easy, but Alan laid there for awhile wondering if he made the right move going to San Francisco. He then wondered if the gangsters knew his real name. They could get that information from the school. However, Paul had their names changed to Drake. To be safe, he thought they may have to change their names again.

Alan thought, *"I should have just bought the ticket to St. Louis. I'll see if I can exchange the ticket in Kansas City. There, we could get off the train and maybe stay a few days checking out other modes of transportation. That may stump anyone tracking us."*

They went through St. Louis and didn't get off the train. They continued on until they reached Kansas City. Alan went to a clerk and told him that he and his sister wanted to stay in Kansas City and wondered if they could get a refund.

The clerk called his supervisor and told him the situation. The supervisor said, "Come with me, Sir, I think we can accommodate you."

They followed the man to his office and he asked for their tickets. Alan handed them to him and he made out a lot of papers. He then told Alan to go to the cashier, and that he would be given his refund on both his tickets and the Pullman.

Alan was elated and after getting his money, he asked if there was a riverboat to Topeka, Kansas. The cashier had taken several riverboat cruises as he liked to gamble. He had never taken the riverboat to Topeka, but he knew they had one. He looked at Alan then Betty Sue and said, "If you're unescorted, you'll find they will not sell you a ticket. There has been some trouble involving children. So the riverboats won't take unescorted children anymore."

Alan thought awhile. He knew he needed a haircut, and there he would ask if someone made up people, like in a drama. The barber said, "Yes, my sister has a shop next door. She can fix you up."

They went next door and Alan said, "My sister needs her hair done, but we also were told you can make someone up to look older. Can you?"

"How old do you want to be?" she asked.

"Her, about twenty, me about twenty-two."

"No problem. Just hop up in a chair."

They looked at themselves after they were made up, and they did look older. They then proceeded to the riverboat ticket office and bought a ticket with no hassle. Their ticket was to Topeka, Kansas where they planned to take a train from there onto Denver.

Alan looked at Betty Sue and she had a large smile on her face when they got on the boat. They stowed their clothes and went out on deck. They were standing at the railing and a couple was near them, and the man introduced himself. He smiled and asked, "Are you on your honeymoon?"

Betty Sue held Alan's arm and said, "Yes, how did you know?"

"It's the way you look at one another. Love just radiates. We're on our honeymoon, too," and his wife clutched his arm.

They had dinner with the couple that night and had a marvelous time. They arrived in Topeka late at night. As they were fed on the boat, they went directly to the train station. The clerk told them that the train to Denver would leave at eight the next morning. They purchased tickets to Denver with a Pullman.

They still had their makeup on and looked older. Alan had a five dollar note in his hand and said, "We're eloping. We love each other very much, but her father thinks I'm not good enough for her. He will probably send men to try and intercept us. Will you keep our secret for five dollars?"

"Put your money away, Sonny. I eloped with my wife twenty years ago. So, I know what you're up against. I'll be glad to keep your secret."

When they were headed for the benches, Alan said, "That should throw anyone off. The riverboat will stump them as we were sold a ticket, and no kid could buy one. Now if they come to Topeka, they won't know if we were ever here."

They hunkered down on a bench and Betty Sue put her head against him and soon was asleep. Alan thought about their trip, and thought no one could trace them past Kansas City. In Kansas City there were at least four different direction they could go and none of them would lead them to where they went.

The next morning they had an early breakfast, and then were on the train at eight. Alan said, "We know Denver. I may get a job there, and we could rent an apartment or stay in a boarding house. That may be the best, a boarding house, where we can eat and sleep. I hope I can get a job. We've spent a lot of money getting here."

Betty Sue said, "I like Denver. We had some happy times there with mom and dad. Oh, how I miss them."

CHAPTER 7

Mrs. Thorton's Boarding House

Arriving in Denver they looked around. They found a boarding house that was run by a Mrs. Thorton.

It was mid-morning and Mrs. Thorton was having a cup of tea. She invited them to have a cup with her. They were very polite, and used the manners Sandra had taught them.

Mrs. Thorton said, "Where do you hale from."

Alan said, "St. Louis of late. We are seeking jobs so we can afford to stay with you, Mrs. Thorton?"

Mrs. Thorton like them and said, "Well, I can use Betty Sue as the work is getting too much for me. She will be a big help. O'Reilly stays here, and he runs a used car lot. He used to have a house, but when Emma died, he sold the house and moved here. I guess I'll have to fill in for Emma now. O'Reilly misses her terribly, but I try to keep him cheered up. I've got him interested in coin collecting. It's a worthwhile hobby.

"My late husband has a fine collection. I never was that enthused until I got O'Reilly interested. He is now an avid collector. He spends most of his time making fine things to hold the coins.

"He lost the boy who washed his cars and serviced them, so you might be able to fill that position. I'll talk to him at lunch. He'll pay you enough to pay for your board and room here and then some.

Alan said, "We are brother and sister and will stay together."

"That will save you a lot. I'll work out a good price for you."

At noon O'Reilly came, along with several others, as the house had eight bedrooms. Only two were empty and one of them would be occupied by Alan and Betty Sue. Mrs. Thorton had to bring in another bed. Betty Sue nearly said something, but Alan put his index finger to his lips and she remained silent.

When they were alone, Alan laughed and said, "You were about to tell Mrs. Thorton that we could sleep in one bed, weren't you?"

Betty Sue said, "Yes, but I'm glad you stopped me. People don't realize we are just one person. I read in the Bible that when a man and woman marry, they become one person. We became one person when I was eight. I will never forget that first night in the basement of Mrs. Gordon's house. All my burdens were lifted off me that night. It was sort of like receiving Christ. He takes all your worries about getting to heaven away, when you confess your sins, and ask him to forgive you, then invite him into your heart."

"Alan said yes, we are one person. I've never thought of it like that. We have a pure love. I, at first, didn't love you like that. I thought of you like a sister, but now I know we will marry, as that is what you want?"

"Of course, I would like to marry you now, but I know people will not except that, so I will bide my time. However, as soon as I look old enough, I want you to marry me."

"O'Reilly hired Alan, and spent a lot of time showing him how to change oil and install batteries. He showed him how he wanted the cars washed and wiped down every morning.

Betty Sue listened carefully to Mrs. Thorton and learned a lot, also. She was an excellent cook and taught Betty Sue. Betty Sue was good at house cleaning and worked hard. Mrs. Thorton was very pleased with Betty Sue.

At night Mrs. Thorton brought out her husband's coin collection. It was interesting to learn about coins. O'Reilly had studied books about each coin, what made them good and not so good. He even had some counterfeits that he had taken in. He told them he would never be duped again, though. He had constructed cardboard holders for the coins. He had a place for every coin in the cardboard holder with cellophane over them. He put the date, mint mark and number made, inscribed below each coin.

He loved to look at the double eagle collection. O'Reilly said, "These will be a worth a fortune someday."

He showed his own collection that were Indian head and Lincoln pennies and then his buffalo nickels. His pride and joy was his standing liberty quarters. He showed the empty place where the 1916 was supposed to be. He said, "I've looked at hundreds of quarters, but I don't think I'll ever find that one. Mr. Thorton has one, and it's almost un-circulated" He showed the quarter to them and it was nearly like a new coin. He showed them how to hold a coin on just its edges so the oil from their hands wouldn't stain the coin.

They were both quite enthused with the collections. Betty Sue said, "When we're rich, I want to collect, Alan."

Alan laughed and said, "When we're rich, I'll buy you a collection."

Betty Sue said, "I'll hold you to that."

Alan just wanted to stay in Denver for a few months. His objective was to throw off anyone trying to trace their steps. However, he could tell Betty Sue was learning a lot from Mrs. Thorton, who he could tell, had formed an attachment to her.

They both worked hard and liked their work. Betty Sue could see the things Mrs. Thorton taught her would help her make Alan a good home.

Alan on the other hand, was learning a lot about cars. He could now listen to engines and tell if something was wrong. O'Reilly had shown him how to look at the exhaust and tell if a car needed rings. He learned how to make a car look its best, and detailed the engine to make it look good. He always thanked O'Reilly for his teaching him. O'Reilly liked that and became close to Alan.

The four of them spent most of their off time together. O'Reilly bought tickets for them to see shows that were playing at the Brown Palace. They all liked each others company.

O'Reilly kept a double barreled shotgun just inside his office door in a space that was hard to see. Alan noticed it and asked about it.

O'Reilly asked, "Have you ever used a gun, Alan?"

"No Sir, I've never even touched one."

"Well, it's high time you learned. After work he took Allen out of town a mile or so, and brought the shotgun. He taught him the safety of a gun, first. He showed Alan how he must take off the safety, then cock the hammers of the gun, hold it tightly to his shoulder and pull one of the two triggers. He had Alan shoot it several times.

The first time it bucked and jammed into his shoulder something fierce. He then held it very tightly to his shoulder and shot. It didn't hurt nearly as much.

That night Alan was putting on his nightshirt and Betty Sue said, "My goodness, where did you get that bruise?"

Alan looked down, and saw he had a large bruise on his shoulder. He laughed and said, "Mr. O'Reilly has been teaching me to shoot his shotgun."

Betty Sue came over and examined it closely. She said, "It appears to me that the one shooting the shotgun gets hurt nearly as badly as the one getting shot," and they both laughed. She stroked the bruise a couple of times and asked, "Does it hurt much?"

"I only noticed it when you pointed it out to me."

"Don't shoot that thing anymore, I don't like you being hurt."

Alan said, "Betty Sue, I believe you like everything on me. I bet you adore my big toe."

Betty Sue said, "I do adore your big toe. I like every inch of your body and someday it will be all mine."

Alan hugged and kissed her and she held tightly to him.

Just a few weeks later, about mid-morning, two men came and wanted to trade for a car. O'Reilly didn't agree to the terms they asked, and told them it was no deal.

The men got surly with him then, and said, "We're taking the car whether you like it or not."

"And I told you I'm not making that deal."

One of the men then hit O'Reilly and knocked him down. About that time a tremendous boom came from the shotgun that was so loud that it startled everyone."

Alan had shot over their heads, but was pointing the gun towards them and said, "I still have a barrel for you, if you don't get back in your car and leave at once.

One of the men said, "You won't use that gun on us, Sonny," and pulled his own gun. Alan pointed just between the two men and pulled the trigger. It knocked both men down. By this time O'Reilly was on his feet and grabbed the man's gun that had fallen to the ground when the man was shot.

O'Reilly said to the men, "Get on your feet if you can, we're going to the sheriff's office. As he was talking, Alan was reloading the shotgun. One of the men got to his feet, but the other had many pellets in him and was examining his wounds.

The man standing said, "We need to get Silas to a doctor, and I need one, too."

The doctor's office was close, so they went on foot. Doc Leland examined their wounds and began working on them.

O'Reilly whispered to Alan, "Go get the sheriff."

Alan left and went for the sheriff. He explained what had happened, and the sheriff took Alan back to the doctors in his patrol car. The sheriff had to make some arrangements for him being out of the office, and it took about ten minutes to accomplish that. When they arrived, the two men were gone and the doctor was treating O'Reilly for a large bump on his head.

The doctor said, "Just after you left, one of them hit O'Reilly and knocked him out. I had finished taking most of the pellets out of the one, but the other hit O'Reilly and they both left. I watched them go back to your lot and they drove away in a car."

The sheriff said, "I'll go after them when I get Deputy Saunders. He then left.

As O'Reilly was walking back to the car lot, O'Reilly said, "That was a mighty brave thing you did, Alan. It took inner courage that is only possessed by a brave man. I didn't think you had it in you, but I now see you in a different light. You became a man today, and a mighty fine man, I see."

"Please don't tell the women about this. It would only scare them."

"You always put others before yourself, Alan. That's another characteristic I admire. I hope you will spend your life here. I'll make you a partner after a few years. I see the four of us as a family."

They all were close, and did many things together.

After the eighth month, Alan said, "Betty Sue, it's time to move on. Our eventual destination is San Francisco."

They explained to Mrs. Thorton and O'Reilly that they needed to get back home. Alan told them they were going back to Chicago to see some relatives.

Alan said, "We will never forget you. It has been a pleasant year. We'll be back someday, I promise."

At work the last day, O'Reilly brought out a derringer. He showed it to Alan and said, "My mother gave me this before she died. I have kept it oiled and in good shape. I want you to have it, Alan. I hope you never have to use it, but its not safe now, with all the riffraff and trash you see. Wipe it down every month or so. I have a box of shells for it. I want you to fire it a couple of times. It's alright to fire it at the back wall."

Alan took the derringer, took of the safety and fired at the back wall. He fired again and said, "Thank you, I see it will be easy to hide."

They said there goodbyes. Mrs. Thorton was in tears and O'Reilly looked very sad. Betty Sue turned to Mr. O'Reilly and said, "You ought to marry Mrs. Thorton. People who like each other should be together. Mrs. Thorton turned red, but O'Reilly said, "I promise you, I will look into that."

When Alan and Betty Sue left, O'Reilly turned to Mrs. Thorton and said, "Out of the mouths of babes comes wisdom. What do you say Mrs. Thorton, could you put up with an old coot like me?"

She smiled and said, "I thought you would never ask. We shall hold Betty Sue dear to our hearts forever. I don't think we would have ever gotten together without her. She has more love in her heart than an angel."

O'Reilly said, "Yes, and most of it is for Alan. It's hard to believe they're brother and sister the way they look at one another. It's not sensual, it's pure love."

"That is what I saw, too."

On the train Alan showed Betty Sue the derringer. She gasped and asked, "Where did you get that, Alan?"

"O'Reilly gave it to me as a parting gift. He showed me how to use it. I'm going to show you how to use it. You see this button, that's the safety. The gun won't fire with that on. However, just pull it back, and the gun is ready to fire. To reload it, just break it apart like this, and put in the bullets. Simple isn't it?"

Betty Sue said, "Why are you showing me all this, Alan?"

"Because I want you to carry it. No one would ever suspect you having a gun. They would suspect me and search me. Could you use it to save our lives?"

"I could empty the gun on anyone who tried to touch you, Alan."

"Practice taking off the safety and firing it. I have removed the bullets, and I want you to get familiar with it."

Betty Sue practiced several times. Alan could tell she liked handling it. Betty Sue asked, "If I have to shoot, where do I aim?"

"I asked O'Reilly that same question. He said aim at the center of the man's chest."

She practiced a few more times, then loaded it, put the safety on, then put it in a deep pocket of her dress.

"She said, "I feel safer now. If any women tries to come on to you, they may feel the wrath of this pistol," and Alan laughed.

CHAPTER 8

The Revenge

After Kyle had the kids where he thought they were safe, he knew it was time to attend to Mr. O'Banion. He returned to Springfield to get enough money from the bank to last him awhile. He then drove to Chicago. He disguised himself by letting his beard and mustache grow since the murder. He wore clothes that older men wore and a homburg hat that he kept pulled down to his eyes. He was nicely dressed, but he had changed his looks considerably. He rented a room in an upscale apartment just across the street from Dion's building. He then began his plot of revenge.

He wrote Dion a letter. It read:

Dion,

I would have returned your hundred-thousand, but now that you had my wife raped and murdered, I will now do the same to your wife and children. I may wait five years to do this or do it next week. You will never know when. I will also take the men who did this and burn them alive. My only aim in life now is to hurt you, your men and organization and you know I have your money to do it with.

Your worst nightmare

When Dion received the letter, he was furious. He called in four of his closest men and said, "Crowley and Grover have done something to me that I must tend to. I'm going to call them in. Be ready to kill them if I touch my nose."

He called Crowley and Grover in and handed them the letter.

Crowley looked up and said, "We only did what you would have done."

"Yes, maybe, but you did it without permission. Now, you've put my family in danger. Do you have families?" Both shook their heads. "If anything happens to my family, you will both rue the day you were born."

"What can we do, we can't guard them day and night."

"I don't care what you do, but you had better hope nothing happens to any of them."

"We can't live like that, boss. Let's talk this out."

"You are both dismissed. Keep away from me for awhile. I can't stand to look at you. I'll think this out, but right now, I can't see you have much of a future. I may change my mind after this wears off a bit, but I will repeat, if anything happens to Fannie or any of our children, you will be sorry your fathers ever had sex with your mothers."

Crowley and Grover went to a bar to discuss this. Crowley said, "There is just one solution to this."

Grover said, "Kill Allen?"

"No, you idiot. Kill Dion. If someone raped your wife and killed her what would you do? Allen has over a hundred-thousand to live on, and a heart that is full of anger and revenge. Now, we have two people after us and neither one will let up until this is resolved.

"I think we should kill Dion, then go to California and start over. We might even start a detective agency out there."

"That sounds okay, but Dion has a large organization."

"How many will miss him if he's killed?"

"Just his family, but he probably has them fixed with cash, should something happen to him. How do you want to go about this?"

"I would like to make it look like an accident or maybe make it look like a hit from that Italian mob. I'll have to think about it for awhile."

"Don't think too long, something might happen to his wife or kids."

Crowley came up with a plan. Dion was driven home each day. He would leave his building and walk about twenty feet to his car. He generally had two or three of his bodyguards with him to shield him, should someone try to ambush him. There had been some bad blood, as Dion had encroached on the Italian gang's turf. The other gang leader had a maroon Duisenberg automobile. It was always highly polished. Everyone knew it when they saw it. Crowley and Grover found another Duisenberg and had it painted exactly like the gang leader's car. They picked a time when Dion was leaving the building. They roared up to the building with two machineguns blazing. However, his bodyguards were alert and a terrific gun battle occurred. Dion was lying in a pool of blood. His abdomen had been riddled with bullets. Both Crowley and Grover were dead with bullet wounds to the head.

Paul had taken a room across the street just to observe Dion's comings and goings. He saw the whole thing occur. The cops would be coming soon, so Paul came down and walked up to Dion. Dion was lucid and Paul said, "I guess we're even now. You won't need your money where you're going. Dion tried to say something, but then his eyes became fixed as he was dead.

A thought crossed Paul's mind and he went back across the street where a clothing store was located. He asked, "Do you have a large valise for sale?"

The clerk smiled and showed him what he had. Paul picked one out and bought it. He walked back across the street into Dion's building. By this time the police were arriving. The guard at the outside door had disappeared, so Paul just walked in. The guard at the door of Dion's office was still there and asked excitedly, "What happened?"

Paul said, Dion was ambushed and killed. I think it's a good time to get what money we can, and get out of here before the police come in here and confiscate it all.

The guard said, "I agree."

They both went in and opened all the boxes. Paul said, "You take all the twenties and I'll take the other bills. The guard nodded and they began sorting out the money. Paul now had well over two hundred thousand and his valise was full. The guard said, "I'll take one box and see if I can come back for the rest."

Paul said, "There are a million cops out front, let's go upstairs and go down the fire escape at the back." They did and were now in the alley. Paul left for one end and the guard the other. Paul went back to his apartment and picked up another valise and put his clothes in it. He dropped by the managers apartment and said, "I have to leave in a hurry. You can rent my apartment, because I won't be back."

"You have to the end of the month. You have some money coming."

"No, that's a gift to you. Tell the owner you gave the money to me, but keep it. You'll have to clean my apartment. I left it in a mess."

The manager shook his hand and Paul took a cab to the train station.

He went back to Springfield and went by to see the police chief.

Alan said, "I went to Chicago and traced down the killers of Sandra. They were killed trying to kill Dion O'Banion."

"Yes, I read about that gang warfare."

"I worked five years ago tending the boiler in O'Banion's building. He was robbed of a ton of money he had hidden in his building. He only discovered it was gone a few months ago. He thought I had taken it, so he sent some goons down to get the money from me.

"They caught Sandra at home alone and did their dirty work. I was only nineteen at the time of the robbery. How could a nineteen year old boy rob a man like Dion O'Banion? It was one of the men who he trusted the most, as it was told to me by one of the gang members after the gun battle. Well, he got what he deserved. I feel I killed Sandra by just knowing O'Banion."

"Don't beat yourself up, Paul. You only did what any normal person would have done."

Kyle went to Jacksonville to see the kids. Letty met him at the door and just handed him the note Alan had left him. It read

Dear Dad,

We love you very much, but I know you were mixed up with gangsters somehow. I can't chance Betty Sue's life. I love her too much. We will probably never see you again, because I plan to get us so far away no one could find us. Don't even try, it would be useless. We could never have a dad and mom as sweet as you. We'll love you forever.

Love, Alan

Kyle said, "When did they leave?"

"The next morning when I took them to school. I enrolled them and the principal took them to their rooms. After arriving at there classroom, both asked to go to the restroom and we never saw them again."

Kyle went to the Greyhound Bus station and the clerk remembered the kids. He told him that the kids bought a ticket to Springfield. This surprised Kyle. He thought that would be the last place they would go. Then he remembered the tin box with the money in it. There was close to three hundred dollars there, and Alan knew it. He would have to have money to travel, so he went back for the money.

Kyle thought, *"He couldn't get far on two hundred dollars. I'll check the train to Chicago and ask the clerk if they went there."*

He drove to Springfield and checked the tin box. The money and Alan's birth certificate were gone. He went to the train station and one of the clerks described them and said he sold them tickets to Chicago.

Kyle questioned several ticket agents in Chicago, but none remembered them. He then sat and thought, *"Where would Alan go? His note said he was going so far that no one could find them. That could be anywhere, but would probably be a long distance from Chicago. I don't think he would go north or south. It was probably New York City or San Francisco."*

Kyle thought of Alan's money situation. Going to New York was less costly, but not that much. If it were him making the decision, it would be San Francisco. He decided to go there, but would check the major cities in between. An obvious place would be St. Louis.

He bought a train ticket to St. Louis. There he went to the riverboat office to question the ticket agents. He learned that the riverboats had quit taking children unescorted. Kyle wasn't aware of that. He then knew that Alan and Betty Sue would not use that mode of transportation.

He went on to Kansas City. He went to all the boarding houses, and some of the cheaper hotels, but of course they weren't there. He checked the train station, and found out they had got their tickets to San Francisco refunded.

Kyle thought, *"They are running short of cash, so if they're not here, they can't go far."*

He spent time talking to each clerk at the train station, but the clerk who had talked to them said, "I'm sure those kids didn't go from here by train."

Kyle didn't talk to the cashier who gave them the advise about the riverboats.

He was now in despair. He had followed his last lead. They could be anywhere. They may have gone south or north.

He decided to give up. So he returned to Springfield.

CHAPTER 9

San Francisco

They took the train to Cheyenne. There they inquired about the train to San Francisco. The train left the next morning, but they bought their tickets through to San Francisco with a Pullman. They decided to get a hotel room for the night. They found a rundown hotel hoping for a cheap rate. It was fifty cents for one bed. The room didn't have a bathtub, but did have one down the hall. They bathed and put on clean clothes. As they were going to dinner, two men stopped them. On man said, "I want all your cash, Junior. Hand it over or I'll make you wish you had given it to me right away."

Betty Sue backed away, and drew the derringer. She removed the safety and said, "If you don't leave, I'll put a bullet in you."

The men were shocked, and backed away a little. One of them said, "She won't use that thing. It's probably a play gun, Bruce. Bruce said, "I don't know, why don't you find out, Greg?"

Greg said, "Little lady if you don't put that away, I'm going to pull you into that alley and give you something that you may like."

As he started forward, Betty Sue shot him in the chest. She then turned coolly to the other and said, "Pick up your friend and take him to the sheriff's office. We will follow you."

The man she shot had recovered some and said, "I'm not that bad off. You shot me in the shoulder. Just let us go. We don't want anymore trouble."

Alan asked, "Do you have a car?"

The man said, "Yes."

"Then get in it, and drive."

The men crossed the street and got in their car and left.

Alan turned to Betty Sue and said, "I would have never thought you had it in you. That took courage."

Betty Sue said, "Anyone touching you had better watch out. I thought I had killed him and was ready to kill the other. No one touches you. No one."

Alan said, "I feel a little safer, now that I have someone protecting me."

Betty Sue then laughed and said, "We will protect each other."

Betty Sue changed that day. She went from a little girl to a woman. She now had self-confidence. Alan could see the change and he liked it. She seemed more beautiful to him, now.

Cheyenne was a rough town, and they were located in the seedy part of it. Alan thought that staying in the best part of town was where they would stay from then on.

They caught the train the next morning. As they were traveling Betty Sue started wiping down the derringer and then reloaded it. She said, "I should have reloaded the minute after I shot. The West is dangerous."

"How did it make you feel after you shot him, Betty Sue?"

"I felt exhilarated. I felt alive and ready. My love had been threatened, and I was able to keep him safe. I didn't think of the consequences. I could have gone to jail, but that never entered my mind. I just knew no one would touch you without paying a heavy price."

"You seemed to have changed, Betty Sue. You used to be this small helpless little girl, and now you're a woman with great confidence."

"Yes, I think that moment in time changed me. I became a woman last night."

"We're growing up too fast, Betty Sue. I don't like you growing up so fast."

"The only thing that really changed was that I love you more. You need me now, where as you didn't before."

"That's where your wrong, Betty Sue. I've always needed you. You're all I have, and are very precious to me. I don't know if I could live without you." She came into his arms and kissed him.

She then said, "I will always be here for you."

They had just the one berth on the train and Betty Sue slept hugging his back all night.

They arrived in San Francisco and looked for an apartment near a school. They queried people in the neighborhood to see if the school was a good one. All said it was, so Alan composed a letter that said:

Dear Sir:

I am ill and cannot register my two children in school, but Alan can give you the details.

Thank you,
Mrs. Reclin

Betty Sue had an excellent handwriting, and could write several different ways.

They had decided to say that Betty Sue was a sophomore in high school, so they could attend the same school. Alan was a senior. He had missed a year through their travel.

The principal opened the letter and Alan gave him the information he needed. They were in class that day. Everyone treated them nicely. They explained they were from Illinois and their father had moved his business to San Francisco. The principal then asked what business their father was in, and Alan told him he did investments.

Betty Sue was quite comely she was maturing quickly and had the body of a woman. She was very popular with both girls and boys. Alan was quiet, so he was mostly in the background. Both were smart, as Sandra had enhanced their schooling by having them read many books during the summer. She had structured their reading so that they progressed quickly. She had a typewriter and taught them to type. They practiced a lot on it and did their homework on it, so they were both proficient at typing. Alan bought a used typewriter the minute they rented an apartment.

Betty Sue was asked by several boys to go out with them, but she just told them that she was going steady with Alan.

She could copy handwriting like a pro and utilized her skill by sending notes to the principal when needed.

There was a special school for art that Alan encouraged her to attend.

Alan was interested in the stock market as Paul had whetted his interested while in Springfield. They could talk for hours about different stocks that they thought were on the upswing.

Alan set up an account for his alleged father with a locale broker, but used his own name. He became friends with the broker, and was soon employed as he excelled with his speed and accuracy on the typewriter. Soon he did most of the office's correspondence. He was good at composing letters, so most of the men working there, as well as the owner, would give Alan the details of what they wanted to say, then Alan would write the letter. He learned many things about the business by doing this.

The owner of the brokerage firm was Grady Lombard. He was from the Lombard family which had been in San Francisco for over a hundred years. He liked Alan. Although Grady had several salesmen, Alan was with Grady the most. Grady knew his business and enjoyed teaching Alan the nuances of trading.

Alan had sent in trades, allegedly from his father, with Betty Sue's handwritten letters. Alan was very good at seeing trends of companies, and catching them on the up or downswing. He now had accumulated six-thousand dollars. He shared everything with Betty Sue, and told her that he had put a thousand dollars in cash away just incase they needed to make a quick exit again. He showed her where he stashed it.

Alan graduated from high school that year. He was nineteen. He was now working full time with Lombard's Brokerage, Inc. Lombard could see Alan's skill and they talked at length about stocks. Lombard began following Alan's advise as he monitored Alan's stock, and he nearly always did well at trading.

Betty Sue would paint at home while Alan read everything he could put his hands on about companies, and the market in general. He had studied the commodity market for a year before he bought his first contract. He followed the weather earnestly, and could see crop failures ahead of time, and began accumulating a lot of money.

***

Back in Springfield, Kyle and now Paul, took a job with a stock brokerage firm. He was paid on a percentage basis, and made very little money at first. He thought he could invest better while saving part of the brokerage fee. Being there all day, he began knowing more about the stocks he wanted to buy and sell.

An older man, named Wylie Mix took Paul under his wing and began teaching him some things that really helped his trading. Wylie was quite good at manipulating stocks.

He told Paul, "If you really want to make a career in this business, I suggest that you go to New York City and get a job on Wall Street at the stock exchange. Just don't invest much until you feel you have the hang of it."

Paul took Wylie's advise and moved to New York. He thought about selling the house, but didn't, because he hoped someday to return and find Betty Sue and Alan living there. He told McCarthy, across the road, that he could farm the six acres and use the barn, stock pens and windmill if he would keep the place up. McCarthy was happy for the free arrangement, and shook Paul's hand.

Paul decided to use his real name in New York City as they required a birth certificate, so he was again Kyle Allen. He found a school that taught the principles of the stock market. It was run by a man who had been very successful in that business. He was wealthy and only taught to teach others how to become wealthy. Kyle was his prize student, and Kyle worked hard learning everything he could from the old fellow. That ended and Kyle applied for a job on the floor of the exchange. He found it exhilarating, although at the end of each session he was exhausted.

At a bar near the exchange, where many of the exchanges' employees went, there was also a group of women who wanted to meet men in that trade.

Kyle met Susan Boyle, an Irish woman with red hair. They had several drinks together and Kyle asked, "Why do so many single women patronize this bar?"

"They're hoping to find a husband that will someday be wealthy."

"Is that why you're here?"

"Yes. I've seen how the men from Eire do here in New York and it's not much. Some are in the Irish gangs, but nearly all of them are either sent to prison or get killed. I want a steady man who can provide for me and me children."

"Do you have children?"

"No, I was just talking about the future. I don't want to worry me entire life about money. Take you for instance. I see you wear a fine suit and a silk tie. You look very prosperous. Are you married?"

"I used to be, but she's gone now. It was a tragic death. I lost both my children at the same time. She was murdered and they were both afraid they would be killed, too. I don't know where they are. I looked for a year and finally gave up.

I know I want to be a success someday, and picked the stock market. I'm not wealthy, but I hope that I will become wealthy at sometime in the future."

"You're the kind of man I'm looking for. Do you think the murderer of your wife will be looking for you?"

"No, he was killed in a shootout in Chicago, well over a year ago."

"Well, your children may have found that out and are looking for you."

"No, they don't know who killed my wife. It has been too long, now. They could have gone anywhere. The boy is smart. He may have gone to Chicago just to throw anyone off who was looking for him. He is devoted to his sister. She loves him more than her own life. I wish you could see her look at him when he is holding her. They are in love with one another. There is no sexual thing about their love, it's pure devotion. I envy that. Although I loved my wife dearly, we never loved one another like those two. You would have to witness it to see what I mean.

"Alan would do anything to keep her safe. I know he loves me, but he thinks I'm connected with a bad element, and he wouldn't chance Betty Sue's life for anything."

"My you have made me envious. I want to love like that."

"I think it's a supernatural thing. They have been like that since Betty Sue was eight years old and Alan was twelve. They were in an orphanage after both their parents were taken by the Spanish Flu. It brought them together in a traumatic way that would be hard to duplicate."

"I see what you mean. I could never have that, as my old man would beat me every time he got drunk, which was quite often. Me mother was sleeping with a neighbor. She thought no one knew, but I saw them once from the balcony. I had a pair of binoculars, and was looking around the neighborhood and just happened to look into a window when the sun was just right, and there they were, making love. It discussed me so much, it was hard for me to be with a man for about a year. I put me self through school because I didn't want to be like me mother and marry a man I didn't love just for me livelihood. When I make love to a man, I want him to love me much beyond the lust he feels."

"You're a smart woman, Miss Boyle. I see you finding someone you could love. I have too much baggage for a woman like you."

"Maybe not. Give it awhile, you may find you like me more than you know. If we kissed a few times who knows what may happen."

"That may be true, but I don't think so, at this junction in my life. However, I want to be your friend as I can talk to you. I think we can even help one another. If you see someone you think you may want to know, I will meet him and put him onto you."

"You are a friend, Kyle. That might work both ways. When you see someone you would like to know, just tell me and I will handle it."

They clinked glasses. A few nights later, she pointed out a man who Kyle didn't know. Kyle got to know him and pointed to Susan and said, "Have you ever seen a redheaded woman that pretty?"

The man, Jesse Wright, said, "No, but I would like to know her."

"Give me a day or so, and I believe I can put you two together."

It happened, and Susan and Jesse became a couple. However, three weeks later Susan came to Kyle and said, "Jesse cut out on me. We got drunk one night, and he put the make on me. After that he just disappeared."

"My only advise is, never bed a man if you want him to be your husband. It never works. Once he's made his conquest, he wants to move on to another conquest."

"I see your point, Kyle. I'm not a loose woman, but I have me needs just like a man. I know alcohol does it to me every time. Once I've had too much, I become easy.

I suppose I'm too much like me mother."

Kyle said, "Would you like another drink?" and they both laughed.

Kyle knew that he needed to move on. Most of the women saw Susan and him together a lot of the time. He saw a woman or two he was interested in, but they wouldn't go with him because of Susan.

CHAPTER 10

To California

Kyle decided to leave New York. He studied the map of the United States and decided on San Francisco. The weather was good and he wanted to see that part of the country. He enjoyed the trip across the country. In Chicago, he just changed trains and was off again.

It was winter and everything was covered in snow. He dined well, and met a couple from London. He told of his stay in London and how he enjoyed it. They told him that America was so much different than they had imagined.

Kyle asked, "Where are you headed after you leave San Francisco?"

"We want to see Los Angeles,. Why don't you come with us?"

"I don't have any schedule, so I may just do that."

In San Francisco Kyle was eating at a nice restaurant, and as he was paying out, Alan and Betty Sue were going in. They never saw one another.

After three days of sight seeing, Kyle accompanied the couple to Los Angeles. He liked the weather there, and decided he might just stay there. The couple he had met decided they wanted to see Australia, so Kyle saw them to their ship.

Kyle investigated the brokerage firms, and found one he liked. He decided to follow some of the brokers to their watering hole, and get to know them before he looked for a job.

***

"When Betty Sue turned fifteen, Alan asked what she wanted for her birthday.

She turned to him and said, "I want a wedding ring. It's time we married. I want to be Mrs. Alan Reclin, not just Betty Sue Reclin."

Alan said, "If that is what you want, Betty Sue, you shall be Mrs. Alan Reclin. I could never love another woman. You are very dear to me, and I love you with all my heart." Betty Sue came into his arms and said, "I know that, Alan. God put us together after he took our parents. I want to quit school as I've gotten everything I need from it. I want to concentrate on my art.

"An elderly man gave a lecture at school yesterday. I could see that he really knows painting. I asked him if he would be my private teacher. He said he would, but that he would have to charge me some, as he has very little money. I told him I would have to clear it with my husband. He was shocked and said, 'How old are you?' and I told him eighteen. That seemed to satisfy him."

"How much does he want. Betty Sue?"

"Ten dollars a week. I know it's expensive, but he's worth it."

"That's not much for what you'll gain from him. How old is he?"

"He looks to be seventy, but you never know. He told me he studied in France with some of the noted impressionists. I asked him to show me some of his works, which he did. They were very good. He knows how to blend colors like I've never seen the like. He's better than I will ever be."

"I don't know about that."

They acquired a marriage license and lied about Betty Sue's age. They were married by a young minister who charged them two dollars. Betty Sue said, "I feel safer somehow. At the marriage ceremony I again had that feeling that I got when I saw you at the top of the stairs in the orphanage. The love I felt then saturated me. I felt the same when you said, "I do.""

"I think gratitude had a lot to do with it."

"Yes, but it was much deeper than that. I feel safer, and that makes me love you more. Just knowing how much you love me is part of it, too. Will you be uncomfortable making love to me?"

"Probably. For so many years I have tried to look you like a sister. It was hard when you began looking like a woman, but I pushed that out of my mind as much as I could, because I loved you and didn't want anything bad to happen to you.

That night she said to Alan, "Just follow my instructions and you will be alright. Put on your nightshirt as you always do. I will come into your arms and give you kisses on the mouth, now. I always wanted you to kiss me that way, but you never would. "Oh! I just remembered. You promised me I could see your erection when we were married. I want to see it."

Alan laughed and said, "You never cease to amaze me, Betty Sue. I'm not sure I can have erection after you said that."

"Just lay on your back and let me play with it a few minutes. I think I can make it stand up. Let's just turn off the lights and let nature take it's course."

"Okay, but sometime I want to see it." Alan just shook his head and turned off the lights.

The next morning as she was making breakfast, she said, "Just think we might have made a baby last night. I hope we did. I felt closer to you than anytime in our lives. We are truly one person, now. God gave man a wonderful thing with sex. It brings you so close that it makes you love each other more than any other time.

"I even prayed after it was over."

"Alan smiled and said, I guess we are one, because I prayed also thanking God for giving us this gift."

"It is a gift, Alan. Pleasing you in that way makes me love you more than ever. I hope we made a baby. I want a baby, it will be the start of a family. We both crave a family. That's why we loved Sandra and Paul so much. They completed the family we both wanted. Now, we can create our own family. I want our first baby to be a boy, so I can teach him to be just like you."

"I see what you mean, Betty Sue. We will have a family. I want a lot of children. We can make them feel safe and secure, and teach them to love one another beyond everything else."

"Being married is wonderful. Just sitting here looking at you is more fun now that I'm Mrs. Reclin. I knew we would marry, but I never realized I would be this happy. I've always loved to hold you, but putting our nude bodies together is so much better.

Alan thought *"Betty Sue is still such a delight. I want to always please her. If she wants me five times a day, I'll do my best."*

***

Kyle liked Los Angeles. He had gradually put nearly all of his money in banks, so when he decided to stay in Los Angeles he had most of his money transferred there. He found a brokerage firm that fit him well. After submitting his resume he talked to the owner, Bill Williams. They seemed to hit it off, so he was hired. After just a few months, Williams said, "You have a knack for this business, Kyle. I see the trades you make and many of our clients have started following you. Why don't you start a service giving financial advice. I would go in with you and help publish the letter."

"How could we make money doing that, Bill?"

By charging the people for the letter with your advice. If we could get several thousand clients, we could make a fortune."

"Getting several thousand clients would take years, even if we gave out sure winners. What will keep people who subscribe from sharing our letter with other people?"

"We can tell people if they share our advise, it may cause a reverse effect on the stock if too many people make the trades we suggest. People are greedy. I would bet they would not share their good fortune if they thought too many people could ruin it for them."

How would we advertise our letter, Bill?"

"That will be my end of the business, Kyle. You write the advise and I will sell it. I hope it gets so big that I can sell this business and devote full time to research and helping you."

"You are an optimist, Bill. That's what I like about you. Let's go have a drink."

They went to a bar they always went to on Friday night, as during the week they just studied at night. Kyle lived alone, but Bill had a family.

At their watering hole, a broker from another firm, Alvin Dark, had a beautiful woman with him. He introduced her to Bill and Kyle. Her name was Kara Adams. They all sat together and ordered drinks.

Alvin and Bill were talking about a stock, and they seemed to be engrossed in their conversation, so Kara asked, "Are you a stockbroker also, Mr. Allen?"

Kyle nodded and said, "Please call me Kyle and I will call you Kara."

"I like your name, Kyle. It's unusual, so I won't forget it."

"What do you do, Kara?"

"I'm a real estate salesman." It's been a little slow lately, but I did sell a home in Beverly Hills, and that will keep me afloat for the rest of the year."

"My, you must move in the circles of the upper class?"

"Alvin helped me there, by introducing me to a couple of his clients who are in show business. They remembered my name, and asked me to help them find an upscale house. I was lucky there, too. I saw that Jane Dare, had listed her house after her divorce, so I called her, and told her I may have a buyer. She met me for lunch, and we struck a deal. It was all pure luck."

"It took some initiative to call someone like Jane Dare. Is she as beautiful off screen as on?"

"Yes, but she looked older than she appears in the movies. I would guess that she is in her forties."

"You're kidding. She looks younger than I am."

Kara laughed and said, "Those beauticians can do marvelous things."

"Are you and Alvin a couple, Kara?"

"No, we both date other people. I help him some by pointing my clients to him, and he does the same. He's a good person to know. He's with the 'In crowd.'"

"I've never heard that expression. Well, he's not with the 'In crowd' tonight. Bill's married with three kids, and I spend most of my time reading about companies."

"You are a good looking man and you look marvelous in your suit. You should be a model."

"You know the manager where I buy my suits said that. I thought he was just doing what most salesmen do to make their customers feel good. Do you think I could get into that industry?"

"Yes, I think you would do marvelously. You ought to at least explore it. I hear they make a lot of money."

They could see that Alvin and Bill were wrapping up their conversation so Kara said, "Here's my card. Please call me."

Alvin and Kara got up and left. Bill said, "I tried to keep Alvin interested long enough so you could get to know Kara. She's a looker isn't she?"

"Yes, and very interesting."

Kyle went back to his apartment which was only a half-block away. He picked up his mail and then decided to have a sandwich. He was at the kitchen table and had several letters in front of him. All were advertisements or letters from his banks. He then saw an envelope from Wade Ingram, the manager of the store where he bought his suits. The letter asked him to call Ron Hubert He explained that Hubert wanted to interview him for a possible modeling job. It gave Ron's telephone number. Kyle thought about this awhile. He thought, *"What do I have to lose. People in that industry have a lot of money and that money should be invested, and that's what I do.* He then laughed and thought, *"I'm just like Kara. I look for business whenever I can."*

The next day he called Ron Hubert and explained who he was, and was about to go further when Huber said, "I know who you are, Mr. Allen. Wade Ingram told me about you. I want to have a photo opt with you, and see how it works out. Will you come in this afternoon around three. I'll have everything set up, and will take as little of your time as possible."

Kyle agreed, and was there promptly at three. Hubert said, "You do show promise, Mr. Allen. Let me take you into makeup, and have them work over you a bit. They'll make you up for the cameras. Wade Ingram also gave us a suit he wants you to wear."

Kyle just did exactly as he was told. After makeup, he was taken into a studio that had cameras and lighting. They had him stand one way, then another. They had him smile and then look serious. They took about thirty pictures.

Ron said, "I think you did splendidly, Mr. Allen, however, I will go over the prints this afternoon and give you a call this evening, if that's okay?"

That night Ron called and said, "My colleagues and I want to sign a contract with you tomorrow if you're willing. Can you be here at three tomorrow?"

"I think so, Mr. Hubert. I will want to bring my attorney as he's looks over all my contracts before I sign them."

"Is he your agent?"

"So to speak, I just refer to him as my lawyer."

Kyle had met Thomas Briggs, Bill William's lawyer, as he had advised him once before about some stocks. He called Briggs the next morning and explained that he had an audition for a modeling position with Hubert Studios, and they wanted to sign a contract with him.

Kyle said, "I feel a little naked signing a contract without a pro looking it over."

Briggs said, "You are a smart man, Kyle. I'm not into that part of law, but I have a close friend who represents several people in show business. I'll call him, and then he will call you. His name is Sam Goldstein. He's very good. He's low key, and is well known and liked in the business. He charges ten percent of what you make, like every agent, but he's worth every dime, I can assure you."

"Thanks Tom, you are a true friend."

"Yes, and you put me onto two stocks that are making me a fortune. It's good to scratch each other's backs."

Goldstein called about ten minutes later. He said, "I would be glad to represent you, Mr. Allen. Tom couldn't say enough about you. He also says you're making him rich in the market. I'll want to talk to you about that later. My broker gives me the worst advice in the world. It would be better for me to put the financial page on the wall and throw darts to see what stocks to buy." This hit Kyle as very funny, and he laughed and said, "I think I can do better than that."

Sam came by early to pick up Kyle. He had a contract in his hand that basically said he would get ten percent of the money from the contract he signed with the Hubert studio. It also said he would represent him as his agent.

At Hubert Studios they walked in and Hubert met them. He turned to Kyle and said, "I had no idea you knew Sam. He's the best in the industry. He represents his clients to the fullest, but he also has saved me a couple of times. This won't take long with Sam here.

It didn't. Sam immediately changed several of the terms. He shook his head and said, "You ought to know better than that, Ron."

Ron said, "I didn't know you would be here, Sam. I'll have it changed and send it over to your office."

Sam negotiated the contract's price and Kyle was astounded at the money. Ron showed them some of the shots he had taken of Kyle and they did look good.

Ron said to Kyle, "I wouldn't be surprised if Sam gets you a movie contract by this time next month. You're very photogenic. I see a great career ahead of you."

When they were back in Sam's Cadillac, Kyle asked, "Was he just blowing smoke or do you see this going further."

"You have the looks, body and voice. I can see you going a long ways. I know all the studio owners, and will do my best to see that you go as far as your talent can take you. Remember, when you make money, I do too.

"I don't have time today, but I want to see you tomorrow about my port folio. I would like to do it like this; I know what to do about your career in show business, and you don't. You know what to do about my finances and I don't. Why don't we form a pack and you run my business life, and I'll run your show business life."

"Sounds good to me. I think we can do well for each other. However, I will always tell you about the investments I make for you before I make them, and you do the same about my career."

Sam said, "I feel like we just got married," which made Kyle laugh.

Kyle said, "Sam, you're the one who should be in show business."

"No, I tried it once. It's too demanding. It cost me my first wife. I was away so much she found someone she could see once in awhile. We're still great friends. She told me she saw me more now, than when we were married. You'll meet her some time. I wish you'd marry her so I could see her more often," and again Kyle laughed.

Sam said, "My second wife told me that she felt like a whore being married to me. She said she had to have an appointment with me to have sex."

Kyle said, "I haven't laughed this much in a year."

Sam said, "Of course not. You have to do all the homework for all of us who are too busy or lazy to keep up with our finances."

They were now in front of Kyle's office and Sam said, "I'll see you here at three tomorrow. I'll bring my portfolio, and turn them over to you. It will be like shedding a bad disease." He then drove away.

When Kyle was back in his office he called Tom Briggs. He said, Tom, I just spent the most entertaining afternoon of my life. That Sam is better than any comedian I've ever heard, and he's a shark at contracts. We made a pack today. I'm going to handle his financial career, and he's going to manage my show business career."

"You and he couldn't be in better hands. Now you see why I like him so much. The only drawback is how busy he is. I don't know how he had time to be married three times. When he divorced them, they all said how much they loved him, but could never see him."

Kyle spent at least a day a week doing photo opts. He began to see photo's of himself in magazines.

CHAPTER 11

A Career Change

The phone rang, and to his delight, it was Kara. She said, "I just saw your picture in Life magazine. You looked super. I couldn't wait to show your picture around. I know I'm being forward, but could I buy you a drink at Zodies after work?"

"I would like that, Kara, I'll see you at five-thirty."

Kara looked outstanding. She had a figure that every man stopped to look at. She came in and couldn't see, but she headed toward the table in the corner where she had last seen Kyle. He stood, and she came to him and kissed him on the cheek. He pulled a chair out for her, and then sat back on the booth seat.

Kara said, "Scoot over, I want to sit by you."

He moved over and said, "My modeling career is already showing benefits."

She smiled and said, "It should. You're a celebrity now."

"Yes, and I have one person who knows me. I'm really popular."

She laughed and said, "Only one person now, but there will be flocks of women pawing at you."

"I never thought about the modeling market making me popular. I think most women go for what they want someone to be, rather than seeing who a man really is."

"I guess I'm one of those superficial women, but I like good looks."

"Most men do, too. I like your good looks. You have a terrific body. Everyman I see looks at you, and wishes he were with you."

"Yes, most men have sex on their minds a lot. I guess women do too."

"Did you ever have a deep relationship, Kyle?"

"Yes, only one close, but a few that I liked, but never seem to flourish. How about you?"

"Yes, I had a deep relationship, but found it was mostly just on my part as I found out that he had others. Since then, I have concentrated on my career. However, I know my looks helps me there, so I keep in good shape."

"How do you do that?"

"I run every morning for an hour, then exercise. I read a magazine on what exercises I should do, and I do them religiously, just like you study stocks. It's the same thing actually, we're just trying to help our careers."

"Do you want to go out with me, Kara?"

"I want your companionship. I want to get to know you. I think that is key for a romance."

"Is that what you want, a romance?"

"Yes, I want someone to hold and love. I don't want to scare you off, but yes, I would like to get to know you, then love you if that happens."

"Do you want marriage and a family?"

"I don't know Kyle. With the right person, maybe. I'm going to go slow there, as I like my life. I want a career, and I can't see how a husband and family would fit into that. But I do want love."

"I have needs also, but I seem to never be where that would happen. I'll tell you how I met my wife sometime. It was very strange."

"I seem to be the one who is the aggressor in our relationship. Maybe because I need someone more than you do. I would like to go to your apartment rather than be in this bar." The bar was super busy, and the waitress never came over, so they left.

"I only live a half block from here."

Kara was amazed at the size and luxury of his place. It was neat as a pin, because he had a cleaning lady who came every other day. She was good at her job and he rewarded her for her diligence.

Kara said, "Wow! I'm impressed with the cleanliness of your place."

"Don't give me the credit. Mrs. Downs deserved all of that. She keeps my house, does my laundry and keeps things I like to eat in the refrigerator. If she weren't married, and in her fifties, I might marry her.

"Sit down and I'll fix you a drink. What's your pleasure?"

"Just a soft drink if you have one."

"Are you nervous being alone with me?"

"No, I trust you. I just don't trust myself. I haven't been around a man for awhile and you do turn me on."

"I like that expression, 'turn me on.' I've never heard it before. You turn me on too. You excite me."

They now had cokes that were ice cold. They both took several swallows as they tasted so good, and they were both thirsty. Kyle said, "Shall we kiss?"

"Turn down the lights, Kyle, and turn on some slow love music. I need to get in the mood."

Kyle had a nice record player, and put on a Billy Eckstein record. He turned and said, "Let's dance to break the ice."

She stood and came into his arms. They danced a slow dance with their bodies meshed. Kara then pulled his face around and kissed him a slow passionate kiss. She then pulled him close to her.

They went to the couch and kissed some more. After sometime, Kara said, "I need to go, Kyle. I was about to pull you to the bedroom. Like I say, I don't worry about you seducing me, I worry about me seducing you."

"I would like you to seduce me, but I have nothing to prevent a child."

"Don't worry about that, Kyle. Even though I haven't been in a relationship for a long while, I keep up with when I'm fertile. As the boy scouts say, 'be prepared.'"

"I think we need to wait on sex for awhile. I want you and you want me, but that is just the animal in us. I think we need to know each other more."

"What more do we need to know, if you want me and I want you."

She took him by the hand and led him to the bedroom. She said, "I want you."

She spent the night, but was gone when Kyle awoke. She had left about five and it was seven when he discovered her gone. She left a note that said she had gone home to run.

Sam called that morning about ten. He said, "I have an audition for you next week with Warner Brothers. The part is for a good looking man who a woman eyes. He has just a few lines. I will send the script by messenger. You ought to get it in an hour or two. If you get the part, you will be playing Don Reece. I've read the play, because I have another client who wants the lead.

"When I read it, I could see you playing Don Reece. You fit the part."

After he hung up he called Kara. She said, "I needed to run and didn't want to wake you. Thank you for last night. It was wonderful."

Kyle then said, "I have a favor to ask of you. Sam is sending over a script for a part in a movie that Warner Brothers is doing. He thinks I'm right for a small character in the production. Would you come over and help me?"

"I'll not just come over, I'll bring Chinese food. Do you like Chinese?"

"Yes, I'll see you at five-thirty."

"They worked until ten that night, then Kara pulled him to the bedroom and they made love until eleven. She then left.

Kyle discussed his new career with Bill Williams. Bill was as enthused as he was about the audition. Kyle said, "I probably won't get the role, but the experience is worth all the work."

Bill nodded, then said, "There are acting schools that are held at night. If you're serious about acting, I think you should attend acting school. Even if you see acting is not for you, you haven't lost a thing. It will help you in any endeavor you pursue, even here."

He discussed the acting school with Kara and she thought it was the right step.

Kyle said, "Why don't you come with me Kara? I would be happy to pay your tuition."

"No, I thought of that as a career, but I have read too much about Hollywood actresses, and what it takes to make it. Most have to sleep their way into roles, and that's not for me. I like where I am now. I can see making a lot of money where I'm at, as my clientele is growing. I have two more Beverly Hills houses. Jane Dare recommended me."

Kyle entered the acting school. It was hard work. They had much to study. He met several people who he liked. One girl spent a lot of time with him. After class she asked him to have a malt with her. Her name was Norma Parker.

He could tell she was lonesome as she was from Kansas. She had left home for Hollywood hoping to make it big. Although she was good looking, Kyle thought the odds of her making it was a long shot. They were discussing their careers a day or so later and Kyle decided to tell her what Kara had told him about actresses having to sleep with people to get roles."

Norma said, "Yes, I've heard that. However, if you want something bad enough you have to make some sacrifices. I didn't just fall off the turnip truck, Kyle. I know that I will have to do that, and I will, if it takes it. I've been thinking about getting my tubes tied so I would never have to worry about getting pregnant. I don't want a family. I just want a career in show business."

Kyle said, "If I were you, I would try to get a job in makeup, costume design or even camera work. That would get you around the business where you can get to know the people in the industry. It would be something you could fall back on during lean times. I've heard even the big stars have lean times."

"That's excellent advice, Kyle. You are really smart. I want to always keep in touch with you. I think you'll make it. You're good looking, and aren't to anxious as I see some of the young guys are. You've never tried to come on to me like so many others. I like that. Do you want to be more than friends?"

"Let's just let nature takes it's course for now and stay friends. I've seen people fall away from one another when they sleep together. I want you to always be my friend."

"I had a friend in New York City, who was from Ireland. She was a beautiful redhead. We became friends and helped each other in meeting people we wanted to be with. We could talk about anything. It was a great help to me, as I didn't know much about women. She gave me an education without me sleeping with her. She also got me dates with women I could never have gotten on my own. I did as much for her. It really helped. We both knew if we ever slept with one another, that we could lose that special friendship. I would like us to be like that, Norma."

She didn't say anything for awhile and then said with a wry smile, "I guess I won't get you in bed tonight, but I'm not losing hope just yet." That made Kyle laugh.

Kyle got the part with Warner Bothers, and Sam signed all the contracts for him. Sam said, "We have to get you a new name. Kyle Allen just doesn't do it.

Kyle said, "How about Paul Drake?"

Sam thought a minute and said, "That fits. I like it. It has a mysterious sound about it. Paul Drake it is."

Sam got him several roles after the first. All had more lines than his first role. Since being in the actor's class, Kyle could see many things about acting that he needed to know. One director came to him and said, "Paul, you have really progressed. I hope to have you in some better parts next season. You surely have the looks and build. Your voice is also good. I like working with you, as you are professional in all you do. The director was Howard Hawks.

Kyle had not seen Kara for sometime. They had met some on the weekends, but they were few and far between.

It was Friday afternoon and he had the weekend off. He called Kara and asked if she wanted to go somewhere that night.

She said, "Yes, I would like to spend a weekend with you on the beach. I have a client who is trying to sell his home in Malibu. He told me I was welcome to use it when I wanted. So lets go and make love all weekend, and don't worry, I'm not in my fertile period."

They were lying on the beach and Kara said, "Have you met someone? You don't spend much time with me anymore."

Kyle described his relationship with Norma. Kara said, "Does she want to sleep with you?"

"No." Then Kyle described their relationship.

Kara said, "She wants to sleep with you, but you don't want to sleep with her, and probably because of me."

"No, Kara. I just want a relationship where we aid one another in our trade. I think that will be useful someday."

He then told Kara what Norma had said about sleeping with men to get a part."

"Wow, she's really into it. I hope she makes it. She may like sleeping her way to the top. Me, I just want you, and don't want to share. I guess I'm stingy. How about you, would you be upset if I slept with someone else?"

"Yes I would. Even though we might not marry, I would not like it."

"I guess I feel the same way. I like sleeping with you. I was no virgin when we met, but I have held true to you, since. I've had drinks with other men. Alvin mostly. I know he sleeps with two women that I know. He may sleep with more. However, since we've been going together he's not come on to me."

"Did you ever sleep with him?"

"Yes, but not after I learned of the other women. I guess once you've had sex, you won't go long without it. When I first met you, I knew I would probably sleep with you. How about you, did you think you would probably sleep with me the first time we met?"

"I can truthfully say, it never crossed my mind. I just knew you were beautiful and I wanted to go out with you."

They stayed at Malibu until Sunday noon, then went home. Monday, Sam called him. He said, "I was given a script that Howard Hawks is directing. He said he thought you would be good in the role of Billy Murphy. He's the little brother of the main character. Billy's in love with a rancher's daughter who hates the main character. The love affair is a passionate one, and Howard said he wanted to make it steamy hot. Do you think you're up to it?"

"Yes, I'm honored he would think of me. Send over the script as soon as you're through with it."

"Howard wants to talk to you about the middle of the week. He has Mildred Sikes helping select the cast. She's good at that. She seems to know just who will work in the different roles."

Wednesday Sam picked Kyle up and they drove to the studio. Howard and Mildred met them in a screening room. She kissed Sam and they hugged awhile. Sam looked at Paul and said, 'I love this woman."

They then began talking about the role of the rancher and were throwing names out and discussing who might be the best.

Howard looked up and said, "Mildred thinks you are perfect for the little bother and I do too. We have already selected John Houston for the lead. I want you two to work together. I think if you get to know each other, you can both help each other fit the roles. John will be here in a minute or so.

"By the way Sam, how did you and Paul hook up?"

"I have a lawyer friend, named Tom Briggs. Paul here, made some timely investments for Tom that paid great dividends. He asked me to help Paul in a contract with Ron Hubert, as he was using Paul as a model for Ingram's suits. Once I saw him I knew he would be good. He also does all my financial work, so that worry is off my back. I told him that he would run my finances and I would run his career."

Mildred said, "See me right after you're through with John Houston, Paul," and everyone laughed.

Howard said, "I see Paul is going to be in every movie we do, Mildred. Before its over he may be financing our movies."

Paul did meet with Mildred and she asked him to look over her portfolio when he had time. Kyle told her he would then said, "Mildred, I have a favor to ask you." He then told her about Norma. He said, "I'm not asking that you put her in a movie, I'm just asking that you find a job for her. She'll make her own way once people see her."

"What's she to you, Paul?"

"I just met her in acting school and she worked so hard that I though I would try and help her. I suggested that she just land a job with the movie crew and then work to be an actress."

"Are you sleeping with her?"

"No, our relationship is platonic. Just friends."

"I can help you then. When someone is sleeping with you, it can cause some problems. I'll help you. What's her name?"

"Norma Parker."

Mildred laughed and said, "You're too late, Paul, she was hired last week to help in the camera section. However, I didn't know she was aspiring to be an actress. If she's been through acting school, then I can help her. You are a good friend, Paul. This can be a dirty business at times and if you have good friends, it helps. Howard and I go way back. We were even lovers at one time, but better friends. It's better to keep those two apart. I see you have already learned that lesson. Let's stay in touch through out our careers.

"You already made the best friend you could ever have with Sam. You may not know it, but when we were young we were married. He just doesn't have time for marriage. I saw him once a week for maybe two hours. After three years of that, I told him we needed to divorce. He told me that if I would be happier, he would grant the divorce, but that he would always feel I was his wife. What a man. We parted best friends and always will be. I still love him as do two more women he tried to have a relationship with. I felt sorry for them, but life goes on.

"He only sleeps four hours a night. I swear the man will have lived two of our lifetimes before he dies. He loves life. Everything he does he loves. He is smarter than anyone I know. He can see things no one else sees. I think he could do anything if he set his mind to it. He loves people. Like you, for instance. He saw in you a good actor and knew you could make it. If you want to be a famous star, Sam can get you there."

"Are you married now?" Kyle asked.

"Yes, and my husband devotes a lot of time to me. I sometimes think I am treating him like Sam treated me, as Howard has me working day and night while we're making a movie. My husband asked if I were sleeping with Howard. I told him there wasn't enough time for that. He laughed and said, 'I believe it.'"

"By the way how did you get on with John Houston?"

"I could tell in the first five minutes he knew more about acting than I would ever know if I live to be a hundred."

"He is good. I've worked with him several times. He will be the greatest director, someday, that has ever lived. Right now he's in too much demand as an actor. Everyone wants him. He can play any roll. He's another smart man. He loves what he's doing. He knows he could be a success at anything he tried, but he loves entertaining people."

CHAPTER 12

The Reunion

Everyone now called Kyle, Paul Drake, except his old friends. Paul worked many hours as he still kept up with his investing and spent countless hours going over companies or industries he thought were developing a good product, and had good management. He kept up with Bill Williams, Tom Briggs, Sam Goldstein, Mildred Sikes, Howard Hawks and their port folios, and now invested for them. They just called him once in awhile to thank him.

He did take time to write a financial letter, and that took much study. Howard kept him working in roles that weren't top billings as he had told Howard that unless the public demanded him, he was happy acting in minor rolls.

Mildred had put Norma in some movies, and she moved up quickly without having to sleep her way into roles. The three of them got together for lunch at least once a week.

He became fast friends with Howard Hawks and John Houston. The scripts they sent him, he read carefully. He began pointing out weak areas that needed rewriting. Howard and John began to talk about Paul's ability editing scripts, and together told him he had a knack of that. They encouraged him to read every script they did. His acting career was still there, but not in top roles.

Norma had just landed a staring role, and was now gaining some notoriety. Sam was now her agent, and was good at moving her around to get good roles. Before she accepted any role, Norma went to Paul and got his advice. They had a close friendship. Mildred also was a close confident of Paul. With the four hundred thousand dollars that Paul had taken off O'Banion, he had turned it into well over three million.

***

Alan had been asked to be a partner with Lombard. Lombard thought he may lose him if he didn't share his business with him. The business had grown, and they were now one of the most prestigious in San Francisco.

Betty Sue had progressed in her art. Her teacher wanted her to go to Paris. She discussed this with Alan.

She said, "I can't go unless you go. I won't be without you."

"I'll take you to Paris if you want, but I can't stay long."

"How long is long?"

"About six weeks, at the most."

They agreed, and the trip was set up. Alan paid for her teacher to go with them. They had seats together on the airline and Betty Sue said, "Have you ever wanted another woman, Alan."

"I can hardly keep up with you, Betty Sue. I couldn't if I wanted to."

"Yes, I do keep you busy, but I see men look at me, and I just wondered if you ever wanted another woman."

"How about you, Betty Sue? Have you ever had a desire for another man?"

"Yes. I've wondered what it would be like. Am I bad thinking that way?"

"I don't think so, unless you started acting on your impulse. I know I love you unconditionally. However, the Bible tells us that its sin only if temptation is acted upon. You have to guard your mind against such things. Your thoughts are who you are. You love me deeply, so I think you would never act upon your thoughts. Everyone is tempted sometimes, but when that happens, I just try to think of how much I love you and those thoughts go away.

"Jesus said that when temptation comes, he will show you a way out. So always look for that way out."

"My, I'm so glad I have you. You would do anything to make me happy, and always have. I sometimes wonder what we would have done if our parents hadn't died and we had never met."

"We would have been the two loneliest people on earth. I can't even imagine life without you."

"Me either. However, we were never able to have children. I wondered about that."

"I suppose God thought we had enough love, and children would have taken some of that love away."

"That sounds logical. It does give me more time with you. If we had children, we would have less time with one another."

Betty Sue was able to get into a class that her teacher recommended. The teacher commented on her work. He said, "If you were a man, I can see your paintings as excellent, however, women are not recognized for their talent."

"Why is that?" she asked.

"Just the way the art world is at the moment."

"Even if I were better than the best artist the world has ever known?"

"Yes, I hate to say it, but even then."

Betty Sue told Alan what she had been told. She said, "I want to go home. The art world's unfair."

Her teacher decided to stay in Paris. He met an old girlfriend, and she wanted him to stay with her.

As they were flying back Betty Sue was looking at a Colliers magazine that had an ad showing Paul in a suit. She handed the magazine to Alan. He looked at it awhile and said, "It looks just like Paul. When we get home, I'll call the company, and ask if they will disclose the name of the man advertising their suits."

They were home now, and Alan got the telephone number of Ingram Men's Ware and asked who the man was advertising their suits in Colliers magazine.

The secretary said, "Why that's Paul Drake, the movie star."

"Movie Star?"

"Yes, don't you ever go to a movie?"

"No, I haven't had time for awhile. Do you have an address where he can receive mail?"

"I think he is a financial adviser with Williams and Associates here in Los Angeles. You may be able to reach him there."

"I'm in San Francisco, would you use your phone book and look up the number for me?"

"I'll do that, just hold the line and give me a minute" In just a minute or so, she gave Alan the number.

As he wrote the number down, Betty Sue said, "I'm so excited I need to use the bathroom. Don't call until I come out."

Alan grinned and waited. He then called the number. A secretary answered the phone and Alan asked to speak to Mr. Drake. The woman said, "Hold on a minute, I see him going into his office. Who shall I say is calling?"

"His son and daughter."

When Paul answered the phone he could hardly speak. He said, "Give me a second, Alan while I catch my breath. I am so overjoyed, I'm crying. Where are you?"

"We live in San Francisco, Dad. Let me put Betty Sue on before she breaks my wrist."

"Daddy, is it really you?" Betty Sue sobbed.

"Yes, it is. Can you two fly down her, I'm doing a movie, and I have to be there tomorrow?"

"Yes, we'll be there tomorrow for sure. We'll call your secretary when we get tickets so you will know where we will be."

They hung up and Betty Sue cried uncontrollably. Alan held her and she stayed in his arms. She then said, "Call the airlines, Alan, and get us tickets."

They arrived at noon the next day and there was a man in a chauffeur's dark suit holding a sign that read, Alan and Betty Sue in large letters.

They retrieved their baggage and was driven to Paul's apartment. Paul had called Kara and she had a key to his apartment. She was there waiting for them. She was in a beautiful dress, and opened the door and let them in.

She said, "Paul asked me to meet you. I'm Kara Adams, a friend of Paul. He's on set making the movie, *Dark Hours*. He has a substantial role in it. Anytime Howard Hawks, the movie director, calls. Paul goes. They are close friends.

"Just set your clothes in the guest room. Paul has told me a lot about you. He said you would be sleeping together. Are you brother and sister?"

Alan said, "No, we're married. We've been married nearly two years now."

Kara said, "Paul said you may be bother and sister, but would sleep together.

"I was a little worried about that. Did you marry your sister, Alan?"

"No, we met in an orphanage and fell in love. She was eight and I was twelve. However, we didn't make love until we were married."

Betty Sue said, "That was because Alan wouldn't make love to me. I wanted him at ten."

Kara smiled and said, "Paul said you were in love, brother and sister or not. Would you like something cold to drink?"

"Yes," Betty Sue answered, "Do you have a coke?"

"Sure, I'll get them."

While she was gone they took their suitcases into a spacious bedroom and hung up their clothes.

When they were back in the living room, Betty Sue asked, "Are you dad's girlfriend?"

"In a matter of speaking. We see each other some. He is so busy that it's hard to have a relationship."

"Love should not be pushed aside for anything."

'I understand your relationship with Alan. Paul told me there is no greater love in the world. He said he and his wife loved to look at you two from afar and enjoy seeing your love while they watched."

Betty Sue said, "Yes, we loved mom. Dad loved her very much. We had a great family until those men came and killed her. It ended everything. Alan took me away. He said he wouldn't chance my life for anything.

"So how did dad become a movie star?"

"He was talked into modeling for a suit company and got an agent, and his agent got him his first role. His agent, and he are very close. His name is Sam Goldstein. I'm sure you will meet him.

"Paul has many friends, but little time for any of them. When the movie season is over, I then get to see him some."

"I know I am direct, but do you love him?"

"Kara blushed and said, "Yes."

Alan then broke in and said, "Kara, Betty Sue loves me so much she thinks everyone should have what she and I have."

"Paul has described that love to me many times. He said that no one will ever love each other like you two. Tell me about how you first met, and how you came to love one another."

Alan described how Betty Sue reminded him of his sister who died, and how he loved her. When he was about to tell how Betty Sue saw him from the basement stairs, but Betty Sue broke in.

She said, "I was eight years old and terribly scared of the dark. I knew I would die if I had to stay in the dark all night. But then, Alan appeared at the head of the stairs. He had shoved a boy on purpose so he would be put in the basement, also. When I saw him I fell deeply in love with him. No one could ever feel the love I felt at that moment. I told Alan that I felt the same way when he said, He would love and cherish me 'till death do us part. That first night in the basement, he told me that he would be my mother, dad and brother rolled up into one. I ask him to marry me that night."

"I seem to feel that love, Betty Sue. I hope someday to have it, but who knows what life brings."

Betty Sue said, "You have to go after love. When you love someone, let them know it. I don't want to embarrass Alan, but I want him everyday and sometimes more."

Alan said, "I quit being embarrassed long ago. Anything Betty Sue says is the truth and I like her for it."

"You would like anything she does, Alan."

"Yes, I guess so. I would rather be around her than anyone on earth. Just be around her awhile and you'll see what I mean."

Kara smiled as she saw Alan was saturated with his love for Betty Sue. Betty Sue was gorgeous and Alan was handsome. Kara said, "As pretty as you are, Betty Sue, you could be a movie star."

"No, I see they require too much of ones time. I couldn't be away from Alan that long."

"You could bring him on the set."

"Well, then, I might consider it."

"If Alan were a movie star, would it upset you to see Alan kiss and love another woman?"

"No, I would know he was doing it for money, and that he only loved me."

"I'm glad I got to be alone with you two. I couldn't really get the picture when Paul was telling about your love. I do now, and am envious."

Paul came at five. Both ran into his arms, and they stayed that way for awhile. All were weeping. Kara even cried seeing the love between them.

CHAPTER 13

The War And More

They went out to dinner that night at the Brown Derby. The food was exquisite. They had a wine that was good and drank two bottles.

Paul explained why Sandra was killed because he took cash from Dion. He then told of the gun battle where the men who killed Sandra were killed. He told how he searched for them for a year and finally saw it was hopeless. He then went into the stock market.

Alan told how he had profited from the market, and had become a partner with Lombard's firm. He told of their going to Paris and how disappointed they were about the art bias for men.

Paul then said, "Where do we go from here?"

Betty Sue said, "We will come see you and you will come see us. We will insist that you bring Kara along as I have already formed an attachment. If you're not sleeping together, you will at our house, because we just have one bed for you."

Alan said, "That's Betty Sue for you. She wanted to be married at eight. I don't know how I held out for seven years, but I did."

"You got married at fifteen, Betty Sue?"

"Only because Alan held out. I wanted to make love to him when I was ten," and they all laughed.

"That's when mother told me about the birds and bees. I remember thinking how wonderful it would be if Alan would do that to me. However, we were posing as brother and sister, so people wouldn't be shocked with us sleeping together."

Paul wanted to change the subject so he asked, "How is your art coming."

Alan didn't wait for her to answer. He said, "You would marvel at some of her paintings. I have been toying with the idea of opening an art studio in San Francisco."

Paul said, "That sounds like a great idea. If it goes over in San Francisco, I will open one in Los Angeles."

Betty Sue's art did go over in San Francisco and Paul opened a shop in Los Angeles. However, the attack on Pearl Harbor occurred.

Right afterward, Paul was with Kara and he said, "We need to get married, Kara. I know I will be going to war, and I want to know that you are back here as my wife."

She hugged him and said, "I want that, too. Let's have the kids here next weekend, and we will be married."

They had planned a small wedding, but over a hundred people showed up. Norma was there and said, "You beat me to him, Kara."

Kara laughed and said, "I can understand. He's the finest man, I ever knew. He says he's enlisting, but I told him to let Sam handle it, he's his agent."

Sam said, "I know he's going, so I'll see he has a commission in the Navy so he will have his bed and chow everyday."

Sam did it two. He knew several admirals, and they saw that Paul was commissioned. Paul talked Sam into getting Alan a commissioned, also. He couldn't do that, but got him into the Naval Air Cadets in Pensacola.

Paul and Kara were separated, but Betty Sue followed Alan to flight school.

He was sent to Pensacola and Betty Sue went with him. Kara didn't fare so well. Paul was put on a destroyer and he shipped out ninety days later.

When Alan finished flight school he was sent aboard the Wasp as a fighter pilot. He was assigned to fly the F-4U, Corsair.

When Betty Sue saw him off, her last words were, "Take care of yourself, Alan."

Tom Flock said, "She told me to take care of you also. She probably saw what I saw, that you couldn't take care of yourself."

Alan hit him on the arm.

Betty Sue came down to Los Angeles and stayed with Kara. Kara had Sam's number and said, "Sam can you help Betty Sue get in the movies. She needs to be doing something while Alan's away."

Sam knew Betty Sue, and knowing her beauty, said, Let me handle it, Kara. I'll see that she's kept so busy she can't think of Alan." He did too.

Betty Sue had a natural talent for acting. She was an overnight sensation. She liked it too. It took her less than a year and landed a role opposite John Barefield. He had made several movies and was a splendid actor. He was handsome, and they had several love scenes. After one of the rehearsals he came into Betty Sues dressing room and said, "I think you are not kissing me the way you should. Let me show you what I mean. They kissed several times and before she knew it, he was coming on to her.

She pushed away and said, "Don't do that. I have a husband that I would give my life for. Right now he is flying in the Pacific to keep your life safe."

Barefield said, "I sometime let my lust go too far. I respect you and your husband. When you write him tell him that I am grateful for his courage and that I also am respectful of the courage of his wife."

When Alan got the letter he knew who John Barefield was. He thought, *"Betty Sue is keeping the home lights burning,"* and kissed the letter.

Tom Flock, his roommate saw him kiss the letter and said, "My, you do love that woman."

Alan then told Tom their history. When he was through, Tom said, "I love her, too, now. You say she's now a movie star? I believe it. She is sure pretty enough to be."

Since Betty Sue was now working in Hollywood, she lived with Kara. She was required to work so many hours that she was frazzled at the end of the week. Kara thought this was good that she keep busy. Kara worked more hours also.

Being apart increased their love for their husbands. They shared all their letters with one another.

Paul was on a destroyer in the battle of the Coral Seas and Alan was on a carrier. Alan was good at flying, and shot down five zeroes during that battle. After the battle it was known to naval aviators as *the great turkey shoot*. The Americans had twice the number of planes than the Japanese. The navy also had seasoned pilots where as the Japanese had very few. His wingman, Tom Flock was one of the thirty or so aviators they lost that day. It was devastating to Alan.

Paul was in that battle, also. He was wounded in the shoulder by shrapnel and sent to Hawaii for treatment. He recovered, and was sent back to sea, but this time on a heavy cruiser as the executive officer.

Betty Sue was doing another movie. It was another steaming movie with heavy love scenes. Mildred asked her how she was able to be so passionate with the handsome men she played without falling in love with them.

Betty Sue said, "The reason I can be so passionate is that I pretend it's Alan. I want him so much that the man I'm playing opposite of is Alan, so now you know how much I love him."

Mildred said, "I and every woman in the world wishes we could love a man like that. Howard told me he has never seen anyone who could portray such passion.

Kara meantime got the word that Paul was in Hawaii and tried to go there, but couldn't get clearance.

Finally, they both came home in late, 1945. They had a party at Paul's house.

The first night, Betty Sue said, "Alan, I have to tell you something."

He had a questioning face and she said, "When you see the movies I made, you will see a woman possessed with love. The way I was able to do those scenes so passionately is that I made believe the man I was with was you, Alan."

Alan did see the movies and said, "I'm glad I didn't see that when I was over seas, I would have gone AWOL and come to you."

Betty Sue was deliriously happy, and wore Alan out. Even in the morning she was on him."

Alan said, "I bet you made those guys go wild when you made those love scenes, Betty Sue."

She said, "I did that. One of them said his wife had never been jealous, but after seeing the love scene she told him to stay away from me." and Alan laughed.

Paul played in movies with Betty Sue. They once gave him a script where they would be lovers, but he told them he was Betty Sue's father and passed up the role.

Betty Sue and Alan decided to go back to San Francisco and Betty Sue quit the movies. She was tired of her roles as a vamp, and they surely didn't need the money.

Alan regained his position as a stockbroker and picked up his old clients. Betty Sue went back to painting and opened her shop again.

CHAPTER 14

A Gun Battle

Betty Sue still had the derringer that O'Reilly had given Alan. She bought oil for it and wiped it down at least once a month, but never in front of Alan. The derringer reminded her of the coin collection that O'Reilly had shown them in Denver.

That night when Alan came home she brought up the subject. Alan had forgotten the coin collection, also. He looked in the phone book and found a coin shop near their apartment. The next day he picked up Betty Sue, and they went to the coin shop.

They found holders for coins from a company called Whitman. They bought many of the book-like coin holders. They then looked at the coins. Alan asked Betty Sue which type of coin she liked the best and was surprised when she didn't name the twenty dollar gold pieces. She liked the standing liberty quarters the best. They both remembered that O'Reilly liked his set of quarters the best, also.

Betty Sue said, "Let's not buy any coin that is not un-circulated. They cost much more, but they will hold their value. I will buy coins with the money I get when I sell a painting. It's like a saving's account."

"Yes, but you would never sell any coin you buy, even if you were starving."

"That's probably true, but I love looking at them."

They bought several standing liberty quarters. They looked with a magnifying glass and picked out the ones they wanted. All were un-circulated. They saw a 1916 un-circulated coin and it had a price tag of six thousand dollars.

Alan said, "That is probably the best buy in the store."

"Then buy it Alan."

Alan stood there awhile then talked to the dealer, Carl Glenn. The dealer said, I dare you to find another coin this good."

"Alan then said, "I'll take it. It's sharper than all the others. I can see each toe on her left and right foot and the head is perfect. It still has it's mint luster. You get me some coins this good and I will be a happy customer."

Alan wrote out a check and said, "We'll pick the coins up Friday. My check will clear by then."

The coin dealer said, "Are you interested in gold coins?"

"Yes, but we are going one step at a time. We are starting with standing liberty quarters. We are only interested in brilliant un-circulated coins that are sharp. Many are un-circulated, but I want to see the toes on each foot and a full head. See that the fingers around the olive branch are distinctive and the emblem on the shield has the stripes and the top is clear.

"I've got it, I will be very selective. I'm going to a large coin show in April."

"Where is it at?"

"Denver."

"We may go with you if you'll let us."

"I would be glad for you to go. I can get the coins cheaper than you can, as I'm a certified dealer. I will give you a break on each coin."

As they were going home, Betty Sue said, "It will be good to see Mrs. Thorton and O'Reilly."

"Yes. I'm quite fond of them. He saved our lives by giving us that derringer. Do you ever think about the man you shot."

"Some. I hope he recovered and turned his life around."

The date of the coin show was far enough away that they were able to get people to fill in for them.

The first thing they did when they arrived in Denver was to go to Mrs. Thorton's, and now, O'Reilly's house. They were both ecstatic with seeing them.

O'Reilly said, "What brought you back?"

"We came for the coin show. You got us so interested, that we got into it. We are here to see what they have."

"Can we go with you?"

"Sure. It will be fun. We have a man with us who is a dealer. He knows a lot about the business."

"Yes, there is much to learn. What are you looking for?"

"You got us hooked on standing liberty quarters, so that is what we're concentrating on at the present."

They were at the coin show a long time. Their dealer picked out ten coins that were marvelous. The dealer had the coins shipped to his store. He said, "This will keep the robbers off us."

"They parted from the O'Reillys after the coin show. They invited them to San Francisco, but knew they would never come.

They took the train to Cheyenne, and had a layover of ten hours. They bought their tickets and a Pullman to San Francisco. There were several coin dealers with them. Four men had followed them from Denver in a car. These men had found the place where they would board the train, and were waiting for them just before the train arrived. These men thought the coin dealers would have many rare coins in their luggage, and they could relieve them of their luggage, and make a quick getaway.

The four men approached them. One of the men had a pistol that was drawn and pointed it at them.

One of the men opened the trunk of the car as it drove up beside them. He said, "Throw your luggage in the trunk, and no one will get hurt."

The men with luggage were caught unprepared, and all complied, but Betty Sue and Alan. Betty Sue had her derringer out and shot the man nearest to her in the head. He dropped as she aimed at a second and shot him. By this time the other two were shucking their pistols, but one of the dealers now had a hidden gun out and plugged one of the others. However, the last gunman, shot the man with the pistol and killed him.

Betty Sue had reloaded and was now pointing her pistol at the last gunman. He could see she had him dead to rights and froze, and gave up.

A baggage clerk had seen the man brandish his pistol, and ran for the sheriff. By this time the shooting was over. The sheriff was now on the scene. Betty Sue had pocketed her derringer.

He didn't see Betty Sue's gun. He put cuffs on the man on the ground and ordered all of them to the sheriff's office. A crowd had gathered and the sheriff ordered a man to get the coroner.

They recovered their luggage and walked to the sheriff's office which was just down the street. The sheriff said, "Who killed the men at the scene."

Alan said, "I believe our man shot the bandits, and then one of them shot him. It all happened so quickly, I really can't be sure."

One of the other men said, I thought I saw the lady fire at one of the bandits and then at another, but she doesn't have a gun so I don't know who did it."

The derringer was now in Alan's back pocket. The sheriff searched Betty Sue and she said, "Watch your hands, Sheriff."

The Sheriff quickly backed away from her, as he surely didn't want to be accused of feeling her.

One of the men said, We had nothing to do with the shooting, and we have a train to catch, we have to go. So, they all turned and left. They barely had time to make the train as it was ready to pull out.

On the train they sat where they faced the chair in front of them. Carl, their coin dealer, sat in one of the chairs and another coin dealer sat beside him. This man kept staring at Betty Sue and said, "I know I've seen you before. You look very familiar."

"Maybe you caught one of my movies. My stage name is Lara Grey."

"By the name of Lord Harry, you are Lara Grey. I can't wait to tell Suzie that I rode with you on the train."

"Just don't tell her you rode with me on the Pullman or she may get upset."

He turned scarlet, and the rest laughed.

"You'll have to excuse her, Sir, that's the show business talking," said Alan.

The guy said again, "Riding with Lara Grey, she'll never believe me. Would you sign my coin show program?"

"Sure" She wrote: "Suzie, your husband rode with me on the train. (she then crossed out 'with') He rides good, I can see why you married him, Lara Grey."

The dealer didn't even read it. He just put it away in his valise.

***

As Alan and Betty Sue lived in the middle of the San Francisco business district, they never owned a car. They had a space for a car under the building, so Alan said, "Why don't we buy a car. We could go up to Marin County and explore some of that. We've never been to Sausalito, Tiburon or the Muir Woods.

Betty Sue said, "I remember dad teaching you to drive while you were in Springfield, but I need to learn."

They looked up a driving school and she enrolled. She said, "I'm nervous, Alan, will you go with me?"

"Sure, I can understand your apprehension, but I think you'll do fine."

The lessons started and Betty Sue took to driving and loved it. They then looked for a car. They had seen some foreign cars and Betty Sue liked a German sports car called,

Portia. They test drove it and both liked it. Betty Sue loved to shift gears on the hills of San Francisco, so she did most of the driving.

They went to Marin County and saw the sites. They loved the Muir Woods. Alan said, "Why don't we take a trip and see the sights. They began planning the trip.

A letter arrived inviting them to join a Portia Club. The next meeting would be held in Mill Valley where a large park was located. The park wasn't used much so many cars could park there.

They decided to go and were met with warmth. One of the leaders, Hal Dobson, said, "Aren't you Lara Grey?"

Betty Sue said, "That was my stage name, but I don't act anymore."

"My gosh!" His wife, Minnie said, "Please join us. We need a celebrity. When we ask for places to meet, we are often turned down. If we have your picture on our stationary, it will open doors that have been shut on us."

"I'm not sure I want you to do that. I find notoriety a bad thing. You never have any peace in public. Since leaving Hollywood, I finally have some peace. Please don't put me in that position again."

Minnie said, "I see what you mean. We won't do that, Hal. Let's just let them be ordinary members, and enjoy them. She then turned to Alan and said, "You haven't introduced your handsome husband."

"This is Alan. I've had him since I was eight years old."

"You were married at eight?"

"No, but we've been together since then. He held me off until I was fifteen, but then I persuaded him to marry me."

Hal said, "At fifteen, my mother was still changing my diapers," and everyone laughed."

Minnie said, "I can see why you latched on to him at an early age, before some older woman snatched him up."

They were surrounded then by the members and introduced to all there. The last person to be introduced was a man who had been in her camera crew. His name was Joel Denson. He had made a pass on set at her during the war. They acted like it was their first meeting. His wife was there and she met her, also.

As they were driving back from the rally, Betty Sue said, "Do you remember the last person we met. That tall guy with the black curly hair?"

"Yes. Joel Denson. What about him?"

"He made a pass at me one time during a movie. Not just once but several times."

"Oh. Do you want to drop out of the club?"

"No, I could tell he didn't want to act like he knew me, and will probably keep his distance. He was going with his wife then, but while at work he came onto me."

"Did you feel you are uncomfortable around him?"

"No. Nothing really happened, but I could see he was embarrassed. Mildred saw the whole thing and he quit his job and went on with another movie company."

"Like I told you before, I'm glad you quit that business. There were probably many more that made passes at you that you didn't even know about. Some men are such pigs. I'm glad you're out of that business. We can lead a normal life now."

We're probably the only couple in the world that can discuss things like that. You and I have the best relationship in the world."

Betty Sue said, "Yes, I know. I can't wait to get home." Alan laughed.

CHAPTER 15

The Korean War

The Korean War started. Alan was one of the first called back. He was promoted to Lt. Commander and given a squadron to command. He was aboard the Princeton. He had transitioned into jets and was now flying the latest model, the F9F Cougar.

He practiced his squadron everyday in air to air dog fighting. They were then deployed to waters off Korea. They flew sorties everyday, baring inclement weather.

They were given a mission of close ground support. This mission was generally given to the AD Sky Raiders, but there were so many requests that the air boss asked Alan for help.

Alan led the mission with eight Cougars. They could see where the North Koreans had the Marines on the run because of their superior numbers. But his squadron was loaded with napalm bombs and came in low, and put their bombs precisely where need. It turned the tide and the Marines were able to set up a perimeter.

As Alan was making a turn not two hundred feet off the ground his plane was hit by machinegun fire. He had a flameout, and knew he was going in. He rolled out and had no time to call in as he was frantically trying to find someplace to set down. He saw a river and put his plane onto it.

He raised the nose and let his tail section hit the water first. He held the nose up as long as he could and made a safe landing. He had survival gear and strapped that on along with a canteen. He decided to leave his parachute on his back as he knew he would need shelter. His plane was sinking fast so he got out on the wing, then swam to the nearest bank. He was in a dense forest and didn't know where the Marine's lines were or where the enemy was. He decided to move south. The trees came down to the water's edge, but he was able to wade and walk south. He had only traveled a hundred feet when he spotted a canoe. He drew his thirty-eight immediately, as he expected someone to be near.

No one was around and he figured that the canoe had washed away, as it was trapped by some roots. He surveyed the canoe to make sure it was watertight. There were paddles in it and even some cooked rice. He was hungry so he ate the rice, and it satisfied him.

He had a knife in a scabbard and cut a lot of branches to cover him and the canoe, so that it would look like a tree floating down the river. He used parachute cords to tie the limbs in place. Once he had everything in place he started. He held to the shore and moved with the current only paddling occasionally to keep his position in the river.

About an hour later he heard voices, so he went into a small inlet and waited. In a few minutes he saw a longboat being paddled by Koreans. He had no idea if they were North or South Koreans, so he let them pass. After they were a hundred yards past him, he moved out into the current again.

He heard nothing for the next three hours, and just went with the current, paddling every so often. He had no idea how many miles he covered, but when it became hard to see, he pulled into a stream that fed into the river. He found a place where the trees had been cut, so a canoe could be brought up onto the ground. He pulled the canoe up and made a place to sleep. He knew there were insects and snakes and decided to rollup in his parachute to keep the varmints from getting to him.

He found a K-ration and opened it. He ate nearly all of it. He kept part of it for morning. He slept restlessly as the noises of the jungle disturbed him ever so often.

The next day he was off at first light. He had packed carefully and disguised himself and canoe as he had before. He began to paddle more as he was out of food and his canteen was empty. He knew he needed to boil some water that night as he had been warned of the pathogens in the water.

Around noon he heard a motor, and thought it might be a patrol boat. He found a place along the bank and covered himself and waited. As the boat came along side of him, he could tell it was an American patrol boat.

He yelled, but the sound of the boat's engines drowned out his voice. He thought about shooting his gun, but then thought they may just turn those fifty caliber machineguns on him, so he let it pass and continued down the river.

About an hour before dark, he found a place where a small stream emptied into the river. He headed into the stream and after a hundred feet found a place to camp for the night.

He was able to start a fire. He kept it small. He took the cover off his canteen and the attached cup and filled it with the stream waster that looked clear. He still boiled the water. Afterward, he put the canteen in the cool water from the stream and let it cool. He was so thirsty that he only waited until the water was cool enough to swallow. He took small sips and finally put it back into the stream to cool some more. He filled the cup with the remaining water and boiled another canteen full.

He was hungry so he looked around and found a fruit tree. He didn't know if the fruit was eatable until he tasted it. It tasted sweet and good, so he ate many of them and picked others for his food the next day.

The next morning he went back to the river. He had only traveled an hour or so and could tell he was coming to a village. He pulled into another small stream and found a place to hide his canoe. He was at a quandary. He needed to know if these people were sympathetic to the South or North. He spoke no Korean and decided not to take a chance. He ate some of the fruit he had brought then napped until nightfall.

When it became dark he was on his way again. He kept to the center of the river as both sides were occupied. He was now past the village and moved on. He went five miles beyond the village, and came to another village, so he just kept going.

He fell asleep and was wakened by hitting some growth along the bank. He decided to just tie up, and sleep in the canoe until dawn. When he woke again, he saw he was next to a small clearing. A girl of about six was standing there watching him.

Alan smiled at her and waved. She smiled back and motioned him to come. He found a place to hide his canoe then went with the girl. She took his hand and looked up and smiled at him and Alan smiled back.

They came to a shack on the edge of a village and the girl pulled him in. His eyes became accustom to the dark as a lady's voice spoke in English. She said, "Welcome to my home."

Alan could then see she was a Korean woman in her middle twenties and quite attractive. She motioned him to a chair and poured him some water and asked, "Are you hungry?"

Alan nodded and she brought him some rice and a pitcher of water. Alan drank three glasses before he ate. He ate slowly, but it took some effort as he was starved.

When he finished eating he asked, "Is this village friendly to the Americans?"

She said, "Some are and some aren't. It depends who's in power at the time."

"Who is in power now."

"I don't really know. No military has been here for over two weeks. The last who were here was the Turkish army. They were Moslems and no one made friends with them."

"How did you learn English as I see you have no accent?"

"I was educated by English missionaries for ten years, from the time I could talk until I was about twelve. The missionaries were sent away by the French, and I was placed in a an English speaking hospital as I couldn't speak Korean. I had to learn Korean later.

"The hospital closed when I was eighteen and I had to make a living, so I went to a bar and found that men would pay a lot of money to sleep with me. As I am told I am quite comely, I charged the highest price, and then just picked the men I wanted to sleep with.

"A Marine caught my eye, and he had a lot of money from selling dope. I liked him, and he told me he would take me back to America when he was rotated. I liked that idea as my life's ambition was to get to America. I never felt I was Korean even though I obviously am. He took me here to be near him, but he was killed some months ago. I need to get back to Soule if I am to make a living."

"What will you do in Soule?"

"I sleep with the soldiers. It pays good."

"My name is Alan, what is your name?"

"I'm Nyaun Kim. You can just call me Kim, Alan."

"Who is the girl?"

She's a neighbor's child. She likes to stay with me as her mother is always angry."

"How could we get to Soule?"

"I know the way through the jungle, but it's difficult and dangerous."

"I have a canoe. Do you suppose we could go in it?"

"Yes, if we go at night."

Alan said, "Pack some food and we'll leave this evening at dusk."

She spent the next half-hour putting food together. To his amazement she had a large canteen and an army backpack. She stowed away everything that she was taking.

Alan drank several more glasses of water and ate more rice.

They left when the sun was down and went to Alan's canoe. They packed everything and left when it was still light.

They were through the village and made good time. They traveled about eight hours then heard a patrol boat. Alan had given up the idea of approaching a patrol boat at night. He just found a small stream and turned up it. They found a place to camp.

They ate some rice, but lit no fire. Alan laid out his parachute and Kim spread her blanket on it and laid down. So Alan laid down by her and pulled the parachute over them to keep the mosquitoes and other bugs away.

Kim then took her clothes off and was nude. She came to Alan and began opening his pants. He held her hand, and she said, "There is no charge, Alan, I need you."

Alan said, "You may need me, but I have a wife and I cannot help you. I'm sorry."

Kim said, "You're the first G. I. I ever knew who turned me down. She must be something special."

"She is. I've known and loved her since she was eight and could never betray her."

"That's okay, there's a first time for everything. I won't bother you." They both turned over and went to sleep.

They packed up and were now on the river again. Alan was afraid they would run out of water as they were down to the last of the big canteen.

They then rounded a turn in the river and saw a pier. Alan could tell it was owned by the Americans. They tied up to a ladder and climbed it. They were met by a lance corporal carrying an M1. He took them to his commanding officer, Captain Ether.

The captain grinned and said, "I see you made it out. Are you Commander Alan Relin?"

Alan had a smile and said, "Lt. Commander, Captain."

"Everyone has been looking for you for over a week. We could find no airplane and no Commander Reclin. We were prepared to look for you the rest of the war. Your heroics have crossed everyone's desk in Korea."

"They made more of me than I am."

"They say you're married to the famous movie star, Lara Grey. We would look for a lifetime rather than disappoint her." Kim was taking all of this in. Even she had heard of Lara Grey.

"Yeah, she's a looker. When I get back, I'll send a thousand photographs of her in a Betty Grable pose for you guys."

"Whose the gook with you, Commander?"

"Please don't call her that. She saved my life at great peril to her own. She was married to a Marine who was killed a few months ago."

"I beg your pardon, Ma'am. I apologize for my ill manners." He then turned to Alan and said, "What are we to do with her?"

"Her family is in Soule and she needs to get back there."

"I'll see to it, Commander. I first want to get you to a telephone so you can call your wife. They did that and Betty Sue picked up the phone.

Alan said, "Betty Sue, this is your husband. I just wanted you to know I'm okay."

Betty Sue couldn't answer and Alan knew she couldn't, so he just kept talking. He said, "A native girl saved my life and brought me back from the jungles."

By this time Betty Sue said, "Oh, Alan. I have not slept since they told me you were MIA. I can't tell you how relieved I am. Will you be coming home, now."

"No, Honey, they need me. Just buck up. There are many women in the same boat."

"Yes, but I have worried so."

Betty Sue said, "Sam called me and has a role he says was written for me. Howard, Mildred and Sam all read the script and all said they thought of me when reading it. I told them I would do it, unless you came home.

"Sam said he would call the admiralty to keep you over there," and Alan laughed and said, "That's Sam for you. I wouldn't doubt he could get it done, either. What's the name of the movie?"

"A Woman's Love." Cary Grant is playing my lover."

"I just try to hope his wife is there on the set. He might just steal you away from me."

"I don't think he's as good looking as you. I would take you over a dozen Cary Grants.

"I will think of you when I am kissing him."

"Well, have fun and remember how much I love you."

Alan was returned to his ship, but the captain sent him to Soule for R. and R. for a week. He didn't want to go, but Captain Yates insisted. He said, "You may not think you need it, but you do. I got that from the shrinks. I hope they're right."

Alan was put in a hotel suite that was marvelous. He decided to tour the bar district in hopes of seeing Kim. He was lucky, he asked directions to the most popular bar for marines and went there.

There sat Kim with several marines about her. She was dressed in a racy netted costume that was over a silk dress. She was simply gorgeous.

Alan was in civilian clothes and when Kim saw him, she pushed the marines aside and ran into his arms and kissed him. She turned and said, "Go away boys, my husband is home."

That made Alan smile. He took her by the hand and said, "Can you get away?"

"Sure. I'm my own boss. Where do you want to go?"

Back to my place where we can have a couple of drinks and find out whats been happening."

When she saw his hotel suite she whistled and said, "You must be an admiral."

"Not quite, but I'm on my way."

Kim said, "I know it's no use to shed my clothes, do you have something cold that I could drink?"

This made Alan smile. Alan ask her what kind of drink she wanted. She said, Pepsi Cola if you have any. Alan looked in the small refrigerator that was there, and there were two Pepsi Colas. He opened them and handed one to her. She took a long drink and came over and sat near him.

She said, "I want you to take me to America with you."

"I can't do that, Kim. I'm married to a woman I dearly love."

"Tell her I'm your maid."

"She wouldn't believe that for a minute. You're too beautiful."

Kim said, "I guess you're right."

I'm working on a visa that will get me to America. I think I can make much more money over there. I do quite well here."

"Don't you want a family."

"No. Not now anyway. I like my profession too much. I may cool off later, and then think about it."

"How do you keep from getting pregnant?"

"There was a program that came through while the French were here that paid fifty French Francs to women who would have their tubes tied. I was in the front of the line.

I met Leo and he was in love with me, and took me north to that little village. He told me he would try to get me to America, so I went with him. We had only a month together before he was killed. I liked him, but nothing like I like you."

Kim stayed with him until he had to go back to his ship. Alan flew many sorties, and was known for his skill and leadership.

Captain Yates called him into his office and said, "Alan, I am being promoted to rear admiral. I want to take you with me. I can get you promoted to commander and I think I can pave the way to get you a regular commission. With a regular commission you can stay in the navy 'til you retire."

"Thank you admiral Yates, but all I want is to get back to San Francisco and be with my wife."

"I can understand that. If I were married to Lara Grey, I would probably go AWOL," and they both laughed.

"Yes, she's beautiful, but she prettier inside. I've know her since she was eight years old. She wanted to marry me a ten when our mother told her about sex. She came to me and asked me to marry her as she wanted to have sex with me. I laughed and told her we were too young. However, she meant it."

"Is she your sister?"

"No, we met in an orphanage, and escaped from there and found an abandoned farm. We lived there a years and then rented a room to a school teacher by telling her our father traveled and our mother was dead.

"After a month she figured out there was no father, but by that time she loved us and we loved her. About a year later the owner showed up. He let all of us stay. He fell in love with our new mother and we became a family.

"Our mother was murdered and Betty Sue, Lara Grey's real name, and I disappeared, and went to San Francisco. Our step-father tried to find us, but I covered our tracks so no one could find us.

"We were flying back from Paris when Betty Sue saw a picture of our father modeling a suit in a magazine ad. He's Paul Drake the actor. He's the commander of the Endurance, now, and is somewhere near Australia right now. He's probably worth three hundred million. He learned how to manipulate stock, and he's the best at it. He taught me when I was young, and I went into the trade right after high school. So you see I want a different life than the navy offers."

I can understand that. Good luck.

CHAPTER 16

Paul Drake's War

Paul was given command of a destroyer when he returned to Active duty. He was in a battle off the coast of Korea, and put his ship between a Chinese submarine and a carrier. They took two torpedoes and were sinking, but he stayed aboard with a skeleton crew, and was able to sink the Chinese sub. They sunk, and were rescued by another destroyer.

For his heroism, he was given the Navy Cross, and promoted to Commander. He was given command of a heavy cruiser, the *Endurance*. They put into Peal Harbor for repairs. He called Kara and she was able to fly out.

After they were in a hotel room Kara said, "I didn't realize I loved you so much until you went to war the first time. I think being away from you gave me time to assess our marriage. I found I loved you much deeper than I had thought. I'm not in Betty Sue's class yet, though.

"She's now making the movie a *Woman's Love,* opposite Cary Grant"

Paul said, "I guess their love is on a higher plane than anyone on earth. A love that deep must be sublime."

Kara said, "You told me they had a love beyond anything that you had ever seen. I remember you telling me that you and Sandra watched them from afar sometimes and were awed with their love. Do you think you could ever love me that much?"

"Have you had an affair you want to tell me about?"

Kara laughed and said, "No. I just wonder if anyone could love someone that much."

Paul said, "I bet half the males in the audience got excited when watching her in those love scenes of a *Woman's Love.*"

Kara laughed and said, "I bet her co-star did, too. She's good. I bet she keeps Alan up half the night."

"Well, sex is a wonderful thing. I expect we'll explore that before we go to sleep."

"When do you think they will cut you loose, Paul?"

"When this conflict comes to an end. Now that the Chinese have put their hat in the ring, it may escalate to a would war."

"I don't think so, Russia won't come into it. They'll sit back like they did in Poland when the Polish people rose up against the Germans in '45. The Russians could have helped them, and saved them from the eventual slaughter, but Stalin wouldn't help. He wanted the Polish people to be slaughtered. He'll be the same here and the Chinese know it. They know they would lose without Russia's help. No, this will end soon."

It did end with a cease fire. No treaty was signed, just a neutral zone established. Alan was let go nearly immediately because of Admiral Yates, but they held Paul hoping they could convince him to stay in.

***

When Alan came home, Betty Sue took him to see *A Woman's Love*. After the movie, Betty Sue said, "What do you think?"

"I bet he tried to bed you."

"No, he was hotly involved with a young actress. She was on the set everyday and took him away right after every love scene."

As they were driving, Alan said, "Let me tell you about how I was rescued."

"When I was turning my airplane after a bombing run, I was just a couple of hundred feet off the ground. Just as I turned, I came into a blaze of machinegun fire from the ground. They must have hit something vital, as I had a flameout. I had to find a place to land immediately.

"I spotted a river and was barely able to get there. I landed in the river safely and swam to shore. I found a canoe and paddled it down river maybe fifty or so miles. I came to a village and turned up a stream and found a camping place. As I was hiding my canoe a little girl was watching me. She smiled at me and motioned me to come with her. She brought me to a hut where a young Korean woman lived.

"The woman spoke perfect English. She was raised by English missionaries and later worked in an English hospital until she was nineteen. She then met a Marine who brought her to the village, that I was at, to be near her. The Marine was killed a few months before I got there. She wanted to get back to Soule, where she was from. So I invited her to go with me in my canoe. She fed me so I had food for the trip.

"The bugs are thick there. I had taken my parachute so I could roll up in it at night to keep the bugs off. She rolled up with me and took off her clothes. She wanted me, but I explained I was in love with my wife. She took it well, and I had no further trouble with her."

"We came to an army base and they took her back to Soule and they took me back to my ship.

"The old man told me I had to take R. and R. It was not a request, it was an order.

"They put me up in the finest hotel and gave me a suite of rooms. I decided to roam the streets and I ran into Kim, as I called her. She came to my suite and tried to persuade me to take her back to the States. She said I could tell you she was my maid. But I told her as pretty as she was, no one would believe that. She understood and told me she was working on a visa to come to the States.

"I was careful not to tell her where I was from. What do you think of all that."

"I know you love only me she was fighting a lost cause. If you wouldn't bed me until we married, I know she wouldn't have a chance," and then laughed. I haven't had that worry since I first met you."

"Oh! I can't wait to show you the two coins Carl got us. You won't believe it. Of course you won't believe the price either. They were costly, but I had to have them. They are a 1927S and 1927D. They are nearly as good as our 1916. Of course no coin is better than that coin. Carl mentions it to me every time I go in there."

When they got home, Betty Sue brought out the collection with a magnifying glass. Alan viewed the two coins and said, "I don't care what you paid for them, those are jewels. We just lack replacing a few other coins and we'll have the greatest standing liberty collection in the world. When we finish this, what do we want to attack."

"I think double eagles will be worth more in the future than any other coins. They are expensive, but most of them are in great shape. Carl has been trying to interest me, but I told him that we have to make that decision together. I found it isn't as fun doing the collection alone. Looking at coins with you is terrific. I got a great thrill out of showing you those quarters. I look at them nearly everyday when I get tired of painting.

"I have a new manager in our store, and he has become demanding. He told me last week that I needed to assign more time to my painting. I nearly laughed.

"While you were gone I went to an art class and found a couple who both paint. They are good. I have several of their paintings in the store. I have twelve people now who market their paintings there. Also, the manager buys some from the museum when they want to sell something.

"Most of everything I sell goes into our special savings account that we use for coins. That's where I got the money to buy those the two quarters. The savings is nearly depleted, now."

"Yes, but I would have mortgaged the apartment for those coins. Did you notice the left foot, every toe showed distinctly."

"Yes, and the head is perfect. Every hair shows and with the brilliant sheen they are perfect," said Betty Sue.

"Did Carl say where he got them?'

"Yes, he said that one of the old mint directors died, and his estate was selling them. The relatives of the old director knew Carl was his friend, so they asked him to market the coins for the estate.

"He told me that he only added ten percent for his commission to the value he placed on them. He said that the minute he saw them, he knew they were ours. He told me he gets as much thrill from our collection as we do."

***

The next Saturday, Betty Sue took him to a Portia rally that was held in Santa Cruz. The trip down there was fun. Betty Sue drove. The club greeted Alan for his service and he was honored.

They then decided to continue down highway one to Monterey. They rented a hotel room, and ate diner in the hotel's dining room. A man came to their table that Betty Sue knew. He had been in her last movie. They invited him to sit down, and he had dinner with them. His name was Dick Cary. He was a character actor, and was in many of Howard Hawks' films.

During dinner he told about his new home in Carmel. He invited them to tour Pebble Beach with him, as he wanted them to see the area and show off his home. They had breakfast with him the next morning and followed him to Carmel.

They were impressed with both the area and his home. While Dick was showing them his home he said, "It was real lucky to see you, Lara. I never come to Monterey, but my car has been on the blink, and there are no mechanics that service Ferrari around the Pebble Beach area, but I found a guy in Monterey that does a great job."

He was offering them some coffee when a man barraged in the front door with a pistol and shot Dick. He was about to turn the pistol their way when Betty Sue shot him in the head and killed him.

Dick was still conscious and witnessed the whole thing. He was hit in the left shoulder just under the clavicle on that side. Alan was on the phone immediately to the police and told them Dick Cary had been shot. The police asked the address and Dick was able to tell them.

In just minutes the police were there. The ambulance came some twenty minutes later. This gave Dick time enough to tell the police the whole story, and that Betty Sue had shot in self-defense. He was then taken away. Alan got the name of the hospital where they were taking him.

The Police asked them to come down to the station, and they complied. After being questioned for an hour or more, they were released. They then went to the hospital and Dick was in surgery to remove the bullet. They waited, and about an hour later they were able to see him. Dick had not lost consciousness the whole time.

Dick said, "Here's the keys to my house. Just make yourselves at home. I'm sure the police don't want you to leave town."

"Yes, they told us to stay close."

The police then came in to question Dick. They listened. Dick said, "I've been seeing Charlie Mays' ex-wife. They were divorced two years ago, but he won't let it go. He threatened to kill me, but I just brushed it off. A lot of guys make threats."

The officer said, "Well, he won't anymore." He looked at Betty Sue and said, "You hit him directly between his eyes."

Betty Sue said, "I was just pointing the gun at him as I knew he was about to shoot my husband, and I would kill anyone who threatens his life."

"Like I say, you did a good job. I know the district attorney will want to talk to you tomorrow, can you and your husband meet us at the station around nine tomorrow?"

Alan said, "Yes. We will be staying at Mr. Cary's house if you need us. Do you see us in any danger from Mays' relatives?"

"He has a couple of brothers, but they won't know who plugged him until tomorrow afternoon. Where are you from?"

We live in San Francisco on Chestnut Street just off Columbus Avenue in an apartment house. We gave you all that in the report this morning."

"I haven't read the report. Could you tell us how you came to be in Carmel?"

They went over the whole story again and told how Betty Sue had worked with Dick Cary in movies.

The Police left, but kept a policeman by Dick's door. After the police left Alan said, "I see they left a policeman in case the brothers think of retaliation. They know you are in the hospital, so we will be safe at your house."

After they left, Alan said, "We're not staying at Dick's house. I think we should stay at a hotel."

Betty Sue said, "I think that's wise. I like Dick, but surely don't want to stay in that house."

Alan did make a wise choice as the Mays' brothers fire bombed Dick's house that night, but did only minor damage. The firemen were there quickly and were able to squelch the fire before it did much damage. The police apprehended the

Mays brothers and found inflammable equipment in their car. They were arrested for arson.

At the station the next day, they heard about the fire bombing and knew they had made the right decision going to a hotel.

After hearing all the stories, the district attorney's assistant said, "I'm glad to hear you spent the night in a hotel and missed all the activity that went on at Mr. Cary's house last night. You're free to go home. We won't need you until the coroner's inquest and that will probably be behind closed doors next week. You ought to be safe, as the Mays brothers are behind bars.

"You did quite admirably Mrs. Reclin. He paused a minute and looked at Alan and said, "Are you Commander Reclin, Sir?"

"Lt. Commander Reclin."

"I was in the 1st Marine division on hill 368 and you saved our bacon. I always wanted to shake you're hand. You nearly lost your life doing it, and every Marine in our battalion was looking for you for a week until you turned up.

"We never found your plane. It was a mystery how you disappeared."

"I put my plane down in a river. I was lucky to find a canoe and floated down the river at night until I got to an American base. I was very lucky."

"And we were very lucky that you and your flight saved us that day with your napalm. You put your bombs within a hundred yards of us so precisely that every Marine in our outfit would risk their lives trying to save you. You can't believe how privileged I feel to meet you."

"Thank you."

As they were driving home Betty Sue said, "You never told me about that. You just said, you were shot down. That assistant district attorney really showed his gratitude. I'm traveling with an American hero. I am so proud of you, Alan."

Alan said, "That ranks right up there with the two quarters you found," and they both laughed.

CHAPTER 17

The Appearance Of Kim

After their appearance at the coroner's inquest, they felt they were safe. Only a few people were in the courtroom and none of the Mays' family.

They were home and Alan said, "I'm not leaving our apartment for three weeks. Every time we stick our heads out, something happens."

The door bell rang. Alan said, "That's strange. Larry always calls if someone is coming up."

He answered the door and their stood Kim with her suitcase. She came in and put her arms about Alan and gave him a big kiss. Betty Sue was there and said, "I take it you're Kim."

Kim smiled and said, "Alan must have told you about me."

"Yes, in graphic detail. I appreciate you helping him get back to his lines. He said you saved his live."

Kim smiled and said, "I can tell you are a nice person, but have charmed your husband to where he is devoted to you. Well, I don't blame you. He's a great guy. I'm here to get started in America with a new life. I just need you to put me up for a week or two until I can get established."

Betty Sue said, "What do you do, Kim?"

"I'm an escort and plan to establish an agency here in San Francisco. You would do very well in that business, Betty Sue."

"You even know my name."

"Of course, your husband said, "You are the only one he would ever love, so he wouldn't help me come to the States.""

"How did you get in the apartment house, Kim?"

"I told your doorman that there was a lady in trouble outside, and when he went to see, I just looked at your apartment number that was posted in the lobby and used the elevator and came up. It wasn't hard at all."

Alan said, "Larry could be locked out, so I had better check on him. You two can get acquainted while I'm gone."

Larry was locked out, and was grateful that Alan came down and let him in. He had left his keys on the desk.

Larry said, "Do you know who that woman is?"

"Yes. She saved my life in Korea. We'll tend to her, but be on your guard, she's a time boom waiting to go off."

"I can certainly attest to that."

While Alan was gone, Betty Sue said, "I have just the place for you, Kim. We have a friend in Carmel who will want to meet you. He's a movie star and is worth big bucks."

"I knew you would be good to me. I just knew it. The way Alan described you I could tell he loved you more than the whole world. To have that kind of love, I knew a very kind woman would be his wife. I'm surprised he told you about me. Most men wouldn't do that, because most wives are jealous.

"Tell me more about the man who is rich. If he's not too old, I can make him a good companion. I also won't have to sell my body."

Betty Sue, just shook her head. Alan came back and said, "Are you hungry, Kim. I remember you fed me when I was starved."

Kim nodded and said, "I'm very hungry, like you were when I found you."

Betty Sue said, "Come into the kitchen, I have some leftovers, that I can warm for you."

Kim turned to Alan and said, "You have a wonderful wife, Alan. She was telling me she already has a man picked out for me that is rich. I believe she said his name was Cary. Yes, Dick Cary."

"That's my wife. She is grateful for you saving my life and will fix you up with the friend she worked with when she was a movie star."

"You were a movie star? Well, you surely have the looks for it. When can I meet this Dick Cary?"

"Tonight," Betty Sue said. "We have to drive down there as he's recovering from an operation on his shoulder."

"Oh, what happened."

Betty Sue said, "It was a case of lead poisoning. Alan told me you worked in a hospital. You can nurse him back to health and gain his gratitude. I wouldn't be surprised with you're ingenuity that you can be married to him in a couple of months."

"We're driving down there today?" Alan asked.

"As soon as Kim finishes her lunch. Why don't you bring the car around in front, so we can be on our way."

Alan said, "I have Dick's phone number, I think I'll give him a little warning."

Alan dialed Dick's number and he answered. Alan put him on speaker phone.

Alan said, "This is Alan Reclin, Dick. We were just wondering how you're getting along."

"The shoulder's okay, Alan, but I'm lonesome. My girlfriend won't have anything to do with me because of the Mays brothers, and I can't drive. Why don't you and Lara drive down and see me?"

"That sounds like a grand idea, Dick. We are even bringing you a present that will really cheer you up. We'll be there in a couple of hours."

Kim was eating, but she heard the conversation. She wiped her mouth and said, "I'll nurse him back to health. I have just the medicine for a lonely man."

When they arrived, Dick had a large grin on his face when he saw Kim."

He hugged Lara and shook Alan's hand, then turned to Kim, who had a smile on her face.

Alan said, "Dick, I want to introduce you to the woman who saved my life in Korea. She's the greatest at cheering men up. I came to her when I was about starved to death and she gave me food. She gave me comfort and showed me how to get back from enemy lines. She wants to nurse you back to health and I recommend her whole heartedly. Her name is Kim"

With that Kim came into his arms, being careful with his shoulder and said, "I so what to help you, Dick. I have healing powers that will get you well."

Alan said, "Well, we'll leave you two to get acquainted."

Dick looked sincerely at Betty Sue and said, "Lara and Alan, you will never know how I needed a nurse at this time. I will always be grateful to you two."

"And we will be grateful to you, Dick." Betty Sue kissed him on the cheek and they left."

As they were going to the car, Alan asked, "Why are we grateful to Dick, Betty Sue?"

"She's taking Kim off our hands. That woman would be in our bed tonight if she stayed with us. She has no boundaries. I'm serious, she thinks the world is her oyster and everyone else is here for her."

Dick called a week later and said, "That Kim is the best thing that ever happened to me. However, it's hard to keep up with her and her energy. She already hired a maid and a cook. She does know how to take care of a man."

Betty Sue said, "She will make a wonderful wife, Dick, don't let her get away."

"Marriage? I never thought of marriage. If I'm to keep her around, that may be the best thing I could do. Thanks for the advice, Lara."

Kim did marry Dick. Alan was the best man and Betty Sue was the bridesmaid. There were many people at the wedding as Dick was popular in Carmel. They were both happy. A couple of years later Kim became a citizen and both Betty Sue and Alan vouched for her.

They became good friends with Dick and Kim. Kim was so spontaneous that she was fun to be around. Dick adored her as did many of the people Carmel.

***

It was the end of a busy season of making three film. Paul came home and Kara was making them drinks.

Paul said, "We need to slow down, Kara. I would like to do some traveling. How would you like that."

"It sounds marvelous. Do you want it to be just the two of us or should we invite the kids?"

"You know I'm happier with the kids around us. How about you?"

"The trip will be more fun with Betty Sue. She's so much fun. You never know what she'll say."

"Would you care if Dick and Kim came along. That Kim is just like Betty Sue, you never know what she's going to do or say, either.

"Howard is now using her in some of the films where an Asian woman is needed. She's good, too."

"We don't want to get too many, but I know I want Betty Sue and Alan. Betty Sue is better that a good comedy."

"Kim is not far behind her. She's got more energy than the four of us."

"Poor Dick, I bet he has a time keeping up with her, but he sure loves her."

"They may not be able to go. Kim is in nearly every activity in Carmel. They really like her."

That proved to be case as Kim was helping with the opening of a drama in a new playhouse and simply couldn't get away.

The trip was set. They were going to Europe. They would start in London, then Paris and end up in Rome or Naples. All four were enthusiastic about the trip. They flew to New York and spent three days, then took British Airlines on a direct flight to London.

At the last minute, their plane had a problem and they were given the choice of going on an Israeli airline or waiting six hours. They chose the Israeli airline.

They were now aboard and it seemed nice as they were in business class. The plane was less than half full. They were six hours out of New York, when a man with a heavy Arabic accent said, "We are taking over this plane." He brandished a small sub-machinegun. "If you make trouble for us, we will kill you."

There were four hijackers on the plane. Each with a sub-machinegun.

"How did they get those guns on the plane?" Paul asked.

"They may have been planted on the plane before we boarded," Alan answered.

They already had the pilot and gave him a new heading. The pilot said, "We have to land in two hours or our fuel will be gone."

The Arab said, "Land in Paris and tell them that your plane has been hijacked. Tell them if they don't comply, we'll shoot a passenger every two minutes until our demands are followed."

This was relayed to the tower in Paris. Their plane landed, and taxied to a place to takeoff again. A fuel truck came out and refueled them. They then took off again. The pilot was given coordinates for the next leg of their journey. Paul and Alan were seated across the aisle from one another.

When their guard turned his back to communicate with another terrorist, Paul whispered, "If we get a chance at that guard, you hit him low and I'll hit him high. We need to get that machinegun, then we'll see who's boss."

They traveled for another four hours and the pilot said, "We're low on fuel. The gunman said, "You can make Bagdad."

The pilot said, "We can't make it to Bagdad."

"You will or we all will die."

They were over water when they began to flame out. The pilot saw shore and tried to set the plane down near shore. When he was on final approach the gunman shot the pilot. Even though shot, he raised the nose in time to avoid going headlong into the water. Lifting the nose made a good landing and they skipped along the water. This caused the hijacker in Paul's and Alan's area to be thrown into the seats.

The boys were on him immediately, even though the plane was still lurching.

When the plane came to rest, they were still a quarter of a mile off shore.

Paul now had the gun and shot the gunman near them. The gunman who shot the pilot opened the cabin door and Paul shot him.

They heard some Arabic shouts and one turned toward Paul, but Paul shot first, and killed him.

The last hijacker, who was at the back of the plane, started killing people. Paul steps through the curtains between coach and business class and killed him. Now all the Arabs were dead.

While Paul was doing this, Alan made his way up front and tried to help the pilot and copilot. They were both dead. The plane had skidded onto a flat rock that was some three to five feet underwater leaving water almost up to the floor of the plane.

The stewards were having people put on their lifejackets then encouraging them to jump into the water and swim for shore. There were less than twenty still alive. The people in business class with the four of them, filed toward the door with their lifejackets on and left the plane. They were separated from coach, so the steward thought the plane was empty now and followed the passengers into the water. All were now out but the four of them and one steward. Paul had told his people to stay where they were."

The last steward came to business class to check. The steward said, "Are you coming?"

Paul said, "No, we prefer to stay with the plane."

The steward said, "If the wind comes up, which it surely will, the plane will sink. It would be much better to go to shore in the light."

"We'll take that chance. We don't know what the shore may bring. I feel it may be Moslems and if that's true, I would rather sink with the plane."

The steward said, "It's your choice," and he left and jumped out, and began swimming towards shore. What the steward didn't know was that the plane had wedged into a rock trough that held the plane from moving anywhere.

Paul said, "We have to get rid of the dead bodies. Remove all their cash as it will be mostly in foreign currency which we will need. Let's check all the passengers to make sure they're dead.

Before doing this, they threw the four hijackers out the seaward door that Alan had opened. He gathered all the weapons and stacked them on a seat. The others were checking the passengers.

To their surprise, a man who looked in his fifties, had blood all over him from the man beside him, but only had superficial wound where bullets had grazed him. Kara had a wet towel and brought him around. He could speak English, but looked Arabic.

They sat him in a seat, while they checked the others. All were dead and after taking their cash, they pushed each one with the two pilots out the door. They then secured both doors.

Betty Sue was looking out the windows toward shore and the last of the survivors were now on shore. She said, "They all made it, but may be in for a hard time as the wind is chilly and they have no fire to dry out."

Alan said, "The wind will dry them out, but they will be cold doing it."

Paul sat by the Arab and said, "What nationality are you?"

"My name is Ali Sharah. I'm a naturalized American citizen and a Christian." He then produced his passport and handed it to Paul. "We came from Lebanon, but were beginning to be harassed by the Moslems, so we immigrated to America some ten years ago. I was going back to get may sister, who is still in Lebanon. I speak several Arabic dialectic, so I may be able to help if we have to walk out of here. Do you know where we are?"

"No, but if we were headed east. I may can figure out about where we are if there are maps in the cockpit. I imagine we were flying about five-hundred miles per hour and we were airborne for about three hours and twenty-five minutes. They refueled in Paris, but they must have shorted the gas or put water with it.

"That would make it about seventeen hundred miles out of Paris. If my geography is correct, we should be in the Mediterranean Sea off the coast of Turkey, but that's just a guess.

"Alan, try to use their radios, we may be able to send a *mayday*, the batteries should be good for awhile."

Alan left for the cockpit and Betty Sue followed him. The radios were quite different from those in his Cougar jet. He tried anyway and broadcasted over what he thought was the emergency channel. No response was heard. He scanned the whole spectrum of radio channels and got nothing. He turned to Betty Sue and said, "We're too low for our broadcast to go very far."

She was now sitting in the captain's chair and looked out. She could see many horsemen surrounding their fellow passengers. They had whips and were now herding the passengers away.

Betty Sue said, "Look at that Alan!" In just a short time all passengers and horsemen disappeared over a small rise. She then said, "The way those men were whipping at them, they're in for a hard time."

"They must be Moslems, and could see our airplane had Jewish markings on it. All Moslems hate Jews, so yes, the passengers are probably in for a hard time."

They returned to the others and the others had seen what happened to the passengers.

Kara said, "I would rather drown than be one of those poor souls."

Alan said, "Betty Sue would you and Kara check our food and water supply? Dad and I must figure out what we should do."

They girls left for the galley and Paul said, "I think we should stay here as long as we have food and water. Eventually El Al Airlines will trace us to here. I think we should just sit tight until the food and water are about gone. I think there should be a rubber raft somewhere. We will have time to explore every inch of this plane. In the meantime we can go through the luggage. We will also need flares if we hear airplanes."

When they were altogether, "Kara said, "I think we have enough food for about two weeks. However, I think the water supply will run out before then. There are other beverages and we should drink them first, in lieu of the water. When we get down to a few bottles of water, we must either leave or send someone for water."

CHAPTER 18

The Trip

They had found several rubber rafts in the baggage area. Alan said, "That's a great place for them. Instead of being wet, they could have paddled to shore.

Paul said, "I would like to know what the Moslems did with the others. I think I will go to shore and find out. I think I can keep from being seen and will take no chances."

"Now, why would you do that, Dad. You can't help them. We can tell the Israeli authorities when we are rescued where they are. If the Arabs only have horses they can't take them far."

"Maybe you're right, but if I could do something to help those people I would surely like to do it."

"Those Arabs are armed and hate infidels, as they refer to anyone who's not Moslem. I think you would be risking yourself and us, if you did that. Right now they probably think everyone has left the airplane."

"I suppose you're right. I guess I'm just antsy and want to be doing something."

They waited a week and no one came.

They found many things that were useful in the baggage area. They made backpacks and packed up for their trip. They decided to leave at night in one of the rubber life rafts, and drift with the current, as Paul warned that someone could be watching the plane. They tied up the raft of the seaward side, and loaded everything they were taking.

Paul had suggested that they leave at night and drift, keeping near shore, but getting out of the area of the plane.

Kara said, "We may be able to drift to a seaport and not have to walk." They all thought this was a good idea.

As they were drifting Betty Sue said, "You know, instead of this cruise, we would have to be enduring French foods, and floorshows. Aren't you glad that we don't have to put up with that. Here we are enjoying a beautiful cruise watching the stars," and all smiled.

They drifted all night, but had to paddle several times to keep from drifting out to sea or too near shore. They all slept, but kept one on watch to make sure they kept the proper distance from the shore.

The next day, they decided to drift on. Near dusk they began to see lights, then they saw a pier. They paddled toward the pier.

As they neared the pier, Alan said, "Ali, why don't you go ashore, and see where we are and if the village is friendly."

Ali nodded and after climbing a wooden ladder, and was off toward the village. They waited for nearly an hour, before he returned. He said, "We are in Turkey as you predicted. This is a fishing village, and they have no electricity or outside communication. All are Moslems, but they seem friendly enough. I found a place that we can stay. They will accept

American dollars, as they are accepted nearly everywhere in Asia Minor."

They tied their raft securely, incase they decided to drift at sea again. They went to a place that had dirt floors and just one room. They left their things there and sought a place to eat. Ali asked someone, and was directed to a café. It had few customers. The food was goat meat and goat cheese that was not too bad. They were all hungry so they ate it.

Before the sun was up, Alan nudged Ali and said, "We need to find a fishing boat that will transport us to a city. They dressed and were off. They went to a place where three fishing boats stood. They were all about fifty feet in length.

Ali approached the first ship where a group of men stood. Ali asked about transportation, and was directed to a man who owned all three ships.

Ali explained, "I have a group who were lost at sea and need transportation to the nearest place that has commercial transportation."

The captain said, "That would be Cypress. That is fifty miles away."

Alan said, "Tell him we have a rubber raft that we will trade him if he takes us."

Ali explained this to the owner and he said, "I'll do it for your boat and a hundred American dollars."

Ali said, "Done," then explained to Alan the transaction.

Ali went back to get the others. Alan went to the pier, and with a rope dragged the raft to one of the ships. They didn't leave right away, but about nine that morning they were off. They were put off at a pier in Cypress. Their ship didn't wait, and left them standing on the pier.

Two soldiers appeared who spoke English. Paul said, "We are survivors from the El Al Israel Airline that was hijacked. We escaped, and would like to be taken to the American Embassy."

The soldiers took them to his headquarters, and they met with a captain there and retold their story.

The captain had not heard of the hijacking as it was not in the news. He said, "We have no facilities here for you, but we can transport you to Nicosia where there is a consulate."

The consulate made arrangement for them to be flown to Tel Aviv. Ali made arrangements to fly to Beirut. They all said their goodbyes and were off.

In Tel Aviv, they were taken to the Masada Headquarters (Israeli CIA). Masada was given the approximate location of the airliner. Paul explained that nearly twenty of the passengers were taken prisoner by Arabs. He said, "We know nothing about the hijackers other than they were Arabs, probably from Iraq, as we overheard them say they wanted to fly to Bagdad."

Masada knew of the missing plane, but had no idea where to look. They were let go, and taken to the airport where they made reservations to fly to London.

On the way to the airport their bus was riddled with machinegun fire, and a hand grenade was thrown which made the bus crash into a light pole. Miraculously none of them were hit as they were at the back of the bus. The bus driver was killed and several of the passengers were wounded. They all stayed down as no fires erupted from the bus. Others who tried to exit the bus were killed by machinegun fire.

They stayed on the floor of the bus not moving. Then they heard sirens coming. They still held their position. Gunfire of a battle was now occurring. The police quickly killed all the gunmen. None tried to surrender.

They were still on the floor of the bus when a police officer said, "This is the police is anyone there?" His language was in Hebrew, so they didn't know what he said.

Paul shouted, "We're Americans and are on the floor."

The officer said in English, "You're alright now, the Arabs are all dead."

The police wanted them to tell all they could about the attack on the bus, so they went to the police headquarters. It was after lunch when they left the police headquarters and decided to have lunch.

Alan asked the waiter if they were safe in his restaurant. He smiled and said, "Of course. My two sons have machineguns in the back if trouble starts."

They ate a unique meal. No one knew what it was, but they enjoyed it. They then traveled to the airport in a cab. They booked passage on American Airlines.

Betty Sue said, "Shouldn't we could go El Al Israel Air?" Everyone just shook their heads.

When they returned home Kim and Dick came over. Dick said, "Tell us about your trip."

Betty Sue said, "Nothing much to tell. Just the usual crash of an airliner and a bus riddled by machinegun fire and hand grenades. Nothing too exciting."

Alan said, "I'm going to lock us in and stay here a week."

Betty Sue then explained what had happened on their trip.

Kim said, "I'm glad we weren't with you. I had enough of that stuff in Korea.

CHAPTER 19

The Move

The culture in San Francisco was changing rapidly. What were called "Hippies" had now inundated the city. Everywhere you walked there were homeless people who were on the street. None had a job or wanted one. They called themselves flower children. Which meant to Alan, a person who had no direction in life and only wanted to fulfill his or her bodily urges.

The smell of marijuana could be smelled everywhere. This lead many to harder drugs. The city council were of little help as they looked upon the hippies has just misguided children. This tied the polices' hands.

Alan was home from lunch and he said, "Betty Sue, I want to move. The hippies have ruined this city for me. It just infuriates me to see our young people idle with no direction. Most are on drugs and can hardly take care of themselves. The city fathers won't do anything, so I think we should move."

"That's a pretty big thing to do. I have my art shop and you have your business. It will take some time. Where would we go?"

"I don't care, just as long as it's away from here."

Betty Sue studied a minute then said, "I want to go where the climate is great. Lets sit and list some places."

"Before we do that, let's list the things a place must have. That will narrow down our choices. I'll start. Number one would be a community that has some backbone and will create discipline, so that people are not permitted to use drugs and roam the streets like dogs in heat."

"My you are upset. I don't like what I see, but it doesn't upset me that much. I love California, but there are other states that have areas of good weather. How about Hawaii?"

"Yes, the weathers nice, but you have to travel a zillion miles to go anywhere. It would also be too far from Dad and Kara. We will always like to be close to them."

"I don't want to live in Los Angles. I don't know why, but that city makes me think of sin, sort of like Las Vegas. I would like to start going to church and live in a place that they worship God."

"Well lets put that as number two on our list, Betty Sue and weather will be number three. Now we're getting someplace. I think your idea of joining a church is really good. Can you think of some other things that our new place should have?"

Betty Sue put her hand to her chin and thought. She then said, it should be a place that enjoys art. And must be a place you could open up a trading agency. Oh, and has a coin shop."

Alan smiled and said, "We've narrowed the places to live down a lot. I think the hippies have inundated all of California. I had to drive through Berkley the other day and

I nearly got sick looking at what was on the streets. What was a great university now has hippies all over it.

Betty Sue said, "I wonder if San Diego is better. It has great weather and is surely growing. It is also not too far from Los Angeles. They might come up with a great movie I would like to do. The money is so good sometimes, that I can't turn them down."

"Yes, you are good in the roll of a passionate lady."

"I give you all the credit there, Alan. When I'm in the arms of the leading man, I pretend it is you and everything comes naturally. I think had I married someone else, I would have no talent. Now don't get me stirred up, we need to complete this, Alan."

"Okay, back to business. I don't think San Diego needs to be the place. Maybe somewhere between San Diego and Los Angeles. Remember that pottery shop we stopped at in Laguna Beach?"

"Yes, I adored that place. Maybe we should build a place right on the ocean on one of those cliffs that has a spectacular view. Oh, I just thought of something. Don't tell Kim we're thinking of moving. She'll want us in Carmel and will hound us to death."

"I'm glad you thought of that, Betty Sue. You're right. If she had her way, we would be living next door to her. However, Dick really loves her and she him. They're not at our level, but pretty close.

"I once heard a guy talk about chasing his wife around the bedroom. I think in their case, they switched roles," and this made Betty Sue laugh.

She said, "At least Dick doesn't have to worry about gaining weight. She keeps him in good shape. Howard Hawks sure likes him. He's in every move he makes. He even loans him out when he's not working him. Kim has done alright also. She took to acting like a duck to water."

"Let's not tell anyone, Betty Sue, as someone may just offhand mention it."

They drove down to Los Angeles and spent the night in a motel. They woke early and went on to Laguna Beach. The arrived about ten in the morning and drove slowly and along the coast. They saw the cliffs and an isolated area that could be built on with the ingenuity of a good architect.

They did go by the pottery shop and bought some ceramics. From there they saw a real estate company, so they drove to it. They were met by a middle aged man that had a nice smile.

Alan said, "We're interested in purchasing some land that includes the cliffs overlooking the ocean. Can that land be purchased?"

"The man said I'm Larry Paulson. There are some areas still available."

"We're looking for an isolated area that other people can't build next to. Not that we're unfriendly, but we value our privacy."

I know that area pretty well and I think I know a place you will be interested in. However, it has a heavy price of well over a hundred thousand. I'm nearly sure you can build on it, but the planning commission is getting very strict. You would have to show them what it would look like and that will entail an architect."

Alan said, "Let's take it step at a time. Show us the property and if we like it, we can take it to an architect and he can furnish the planning commission with a rendition of what we plan."

"Sounds like a plan. We can go in my car."

He took them to a place that jutted out with cliffs on both sides and in front. It was about two hundred feet wide and was flat on top. Access from the street was okay but would have to be restructured for a driveway. They walked out and the cliff was straight down to the ocean that pounded the cliff. There were rocks that the ocean went under then spouted up like a geyser. It made a noise that both liked. Both Alan and Betty Sue were impressed.

Alan said, "I think we like it, but we must talk to an architect now."

Paulson said, "I know a good one. He too is a bit pricy, but I can guarantee you will be pleased with him. He is very invocative."

He drove them over to the architect's office and his secretary showed them into his office. His name was Don Lindsey. He said, "Hello Larry, how can I help you?"

You know that piece of land that has three cliffs that isolates it. It's about a mile down the road?"

"Yes, "I'm familiar with it because I've had three clients to look at it. After hearing the price of the land and what I estimated it would cost to build on it, they all left.

Alan said, "What was the cost?"

Over five hundred thousand including my price and cost of the land."

"We can come up with that, but we must convince ourselves that is where we want to live. If we tell you what our needs are then you can show what you have in mind."

Larry said, "We need to sit down and I'll show you a couple of renditions I thought up for that property and showed to other clients. It is unique and should be something the planning commission will approve. They don't like gaudy. They like something that fits into the landscape. They have a new planning director who has really turned things around in Laguna Beach, and I whole hardly agree with him. He wants our community to progress, but conservatively with good taste. He has curtailed the urban sprawl that many beach communities have, and has a master plan."

Alan said, "I would like to write you a check to start our project to see what you have in mind as it fits us."

"Write me a check for two hundred dollars and I'll begin. Larry can take you back and you can settle up with him then return and I will have something to show you."

They drove back and Larry had them write him a check for a hundred dollars to hold the property. He said, "I'll bet Don will wow you. I'm sure you will be glad you engaged him."

When they returned, Don had two renditions of structures he had created for other clients. The showed a wrought iron fence giving entrance from the highway. He explained the fence had an automatic gate. Behind the eight foot high fence that had spikes on the ends, were bushes that kept the structure hidden except for the second floor.

He said, "If I'm reading you right, you want seclusion with safety as a prime feature."

Betty Sue said, "Exactly. We're from San Francisco and are moving because of the change in culture."

"You want shed of the hippies." and they all laughed. "I think you will find Laguna Beach quite conservative. The city fathers wants to keep Laguna Beach as pristine as possible. They aren't as strict as Carmel, but nearly. We want our community to be an example to the American way of life. You won't see many hippies as our police force won't tolerate loitering. You'll see signs in restaurants that say shoes and shirts must be worn to be served. Even the grocery stores have restrictions. That's why you don't see any hippies in Laguna Beach unless they're just passing through.

Alan said, "That has sold us."

Don looked at Betty Sue and said, "Aren't you Lara Grey, the movie actress?"

"Yes, that's my stage name. My, my wife and I see every movie you make. You are a splendid actress."

"Thank you, Don. However I'm just Betty Sue to you."

"I can't wait to tell Dorothy. However, getting back to business, I think the planning commission will require a square footage of three thousand feet. I would recommend at least thirty-five because I have some features that will require that space."

"Our apartment is about eleven hundred feet in San Francisco and we do quite well living there."

"But this is a lifetime house. I feel you will spend the rest of your days here. I have features like a concrete stairway on the southern cliff that will take you right down to the water where I will have a concrete pier. I would construct a swimming place there that is private, but still gives you exposure to the sea.

"Your house will have places for a cook and maid to live if you want them. It will have a great room where you enter with a forty-foot ceiling. You will have a library and a formal dining room to sit twenty or so people. There will be four guest bedrooms all with their own bath and a space for sitting in each bedroom.

"The master bedroom will open onto the sea on the second floor. You will have a balcony that you can sit on and enjoy the sunset and see whales at times.

"Does this sound like something you would want?"

Betty Sue said, "I never dreamed of living so big, but we have no children to spend our money on so I guess this house will be our children."

"It surely sounds like what I want. My wife is not only a talented actress, but she is a wonderful artist. She even has two art shops, one in San Francisco and another in Los Angeles. She will need a place to do her art.

"Run out the estimate and we'll go over it and see it is something we want to do. I hope your fee will cover dealing with the planning commission and the City Council."

"It will. I'll mail you a detailed estimate in a week or so. Do you want me to furnish it, or do you want to do that."

Betty Sue said, "We're really not into that and you are. We'll trust you to do everything. All we want to do is bring our clothes and my art. Oh, we have a valuable coin collection so we will want a safe to keep that and some of my jewelry in."

They left and as they were driving, Alan said, "Well, there goes about six hundred thousand or more. I wonder what the taxes and up keep will run."

"We can afford it Alan. Like I said, "The house will be our children. I'm sure if we had a pack of kids, they would cost us much more than that house and its upkeep and taxes."

They got the price from Don in the mail the next week. It was itemized in great detail, and it was more than Alan had predicted. The total price including the land was well over seven hundred-thousand. However, Betty Sue had received much more than that on her last movie. She also got residual payments each month when her movie was used anywhere. *A Woman's Love* was now playing in Europe and it was a smash over there, also.

She said, "If Howard comes up with another movie, I'll have Sam ask for more money. We still have more money than we could ever spend, so don't worry about it."

"Remember, we're one, so anything we do, we do it jointly."

"I love the pictures Don drew of the house. How about taking an apartment down there and get to see the house as it goes up."

"That's a great idea. I'll just run my business by phone. That's all I do now."

They moved. They had very few things, but still hired a mover as packing clothes and personal effects went better.

They were able to rent an apartment within a mile of the construction site. They first explored all the places they needed to shop. Larry helped them out there. He was very interested in the construction of their house and they had him over quite often to have a drink after he closed for the day.

By watching the construction they were able to change a few things that suited them better, but mostly they depended on Don, who was a master at his craft. He too began spending time with them after work.

Alan said, "After the house is finished I want you two to bring your wives and the six of us will have a party."

Don said, "That's a must as Dorothy surely wants to meet Betty Sue."

Alan and Betty Sue talked to their dad nearly everyday. They gave him their new address, and explained it by saying they just wanted to get away from San Francisco for awhile. They visited he and Kara, as they nearly always had business there.

It took nearly two years for the construction. Everything was splendid. The concrete stairs were put in first with the small dock and swimming place. They still like to fish and fished off the their small dock and really enjoyed it. Betty Sue even cooked the fish they caught and always had fries and cold slaw with them.

Alan said, "If we have a cook, I'll bet you will be right in there with her."

"I'm still learning in that department and will probably be taking notes as I like to cook, especially for you. Do you remember the first meal I cooked for you?"

"Pancakes, eggs and bacon. You were only eight. Why don't we have that tonight?"

"It is so wonderful living with a man who adores me. I don't know how other people live with people they don't like."

At last the construction was over. By this time Don's wife had met Betty Sue and with Larry's wife they had a great time.

Alan said, "I would like to invite my father and his wife over. I want just a small party at first with my family and you people. Let's plan it for Saturday. We'll make it casual."

When Paul and Kara passed through the gate, they were amazed. It was still light and they could see everything. When Alan answered the door he hugged them as did Betty Sue.

Paul asked, "Whose place is this?"

Betty Sue said, "It's ours. We plan to live here the rest of our lives. We wanted to surprise you."

They introduced Larry, Don and their wives then showed them the house and the outside."

Paul looked at Kara and said, "There going to get tired of us coming over every weekend."

CHAPTER 20

The Vietnam War

In 1964 the Vietnam War was on. Just like President Kennedy, President Johnson was determined to keep Communalism from spreading. He deployed thousand of troops to replace the French who had now left Vietnam.

Paul was not called back, but the Navy wanted Alan. He had stayed in the reserves and had flown about once a month. He did this from El Toro which was very close to Laguna Beach. He had transitioned into the F4 fighter. It was a much better aircraft than what he had flown in Korea.

Betty Sue was angry that they were taking Alan for a third time. He was a commander now and told Betty Sue that he would probably not see combat because of his age.

Admiral Yates had especially called for Alan as he knew his quick mind and worked well with him. He was sent to Vietnam a week after he had his medical checkup brought up to date.

He was right in what he told Betty Sue. He worked with Admiral Yates planning the air strikes. As the war intensified qualified pilots were now at a premium. Anyone in Naval Air knew Alan was a superb pilot. He was now asked to lead some strikes over Hanoi.

He was on a night flight and his wing was hit by shrapnel. He could not maintain flying speed and he knew he was going in. He radioed his wingman that he had to eject then pulled the curtain and was met by the cold blast of night air.

He thought of Betty Sue. He did not mind dying, but he knew how much Betty Sue loved him and how she would be hurt. He hated that, as he had always taken extreme care of her.

He came down in a tree that snapped and then he was on the ground. He was in total darkness. He decided to just rollup in his parachute and try to sleep, as he new the next day would be chaotic at best.

He thought of what he would do. He knew his chances of staying out of enemy hands was unlikely. Just getting into enemy hands without being killed would be lucky.

Alan woke when he heard a large bird squawking. He folded up his parachute and did his best to get it back in its holder. He used some of the parachute cord to tie it.

He strapped it on then consulted his compass that he wore around his neck. He started out being very cautious. He listened acutely for human voices.

The jungle was so thick it was hard for him to move. About mid morning he came upon a trail. He couldn't tell if it were made by animals or humans, but it was headed approximately the direction he wanted to go, so he followed it. He made much better time, now.

Sometime around mid afternoon he came to a village. He spoke no Vietnamese and didn't know if these people were friendly or enemies. He knew he must have water and food. He had eaten the K-ration that he always took with him in his survival packet, but was now hungry again.

He waited undercover and watched the village. A half hour later two soldiers dragged a boy out of one of the huts and began beating him. It was a terrible beating that lasted nearly five minutes. They then left him in a heap and left the village.

The boy hadn't moved and no one came out of their huts. Alan figured they were all scared of the soldiers. However, he didn't see any soldiers. He waited another half hour and saw the boy moving some.

Alan decided that he would go pick up the boy and take him back to his hut. He now had the boy and carried him back inside his hut and laid him on a mat.

When his eyes became accustom to the dark, he saw a man and woman that were bloody and lay motionless. He checked them and they were dead from stab wounds. There were some blankets and Alan wrapped the two corpses in them.

He found a large olla that was half full of water. He took a rag he found and wet it and started working on the boy to clean the wounds left from the sever beating. He took his shirt off and bathed the wounds.

The boy now stirred and opened his eyes. He could see Alan in his flight suit and showed fear, but Alan put his finger to his lips to signify no noise. This also acted as a peace sign.

Alan continued dressing the boys wounds and the boy smiled at him, so Alan winked at him.

The boy said in English, "Are you an American?"

Alan smiled back and said, yes. I've come to help you."

The boy then looked at the two bodies that were wrapped in the blankets with sad eyes.

Alan said, "Were those your parents?"

The boy said, "No, my aunt and uncle. They kept me. They were schooled by English missionaries and taught me English. We spoke only English when we were in our house.

"The soldiers are looking for my father. He's a freedom fighter. He has a band of fighters that hates the communist and brings destruction to them whenever he can. He is not connected to the Americans as the Vietnamese, who help them, are infiltrated with spies."

"Is it safe to stay here?" Alan asked.

"For now. But we should move tomorrow. I know a safer place where the people are friends with the Americans. We will move when I know it's safe."

"Do you have something to eat, I'm hungry."

"The boy rose, but with some anguish. He pulled open a drawer that had cooked rice in a large bowl. He sat that on a table and brought two small bowls and some chopsticks and set them down too.

Alan asked. "What's your name?"

The boy smiled and said "Nin."

Alan said, "Call me Alan."

"Are you a Christian?"

The boy smiled and said, "Yes. Please say the pray, Alan, so we can eat." His wording made Alan smile.

Alan prayed, "Dear Lord, thank you for bringing me safely into the care of Nin, your servant. Keep us in the palm of your hand and bring us to safety. Thank you for this food. I ask the words in the name of Jesus Christ our Savior. Amen."

Nin said, "Amen," and dished Alan a bowl full of rice.

Alan had a hard time trying to eat the rice with the chopsticks, but soon got the hang of it. He wasn't full, but was satisfied enough.

After they ate, Alan said, "What will we do with the bodies?"

Nin said, "We'll take them outside and then I'll tell the village leader about them. He will see that they are buried."

Alan didn't sleep much that night and every noise woke him. He slept with his thirty-eight in his hand.

The next day was the burial, but Alan never left the hut. He knew that all the village knew he was there, but no one came near the hut.

There was enough rice to keep them from starving, but was not near enough to satisfy Alan. The water was good as the village had a spring.

***

Admiral Yates was notified at two in the morning of Alan being shot down over enemy territory. Bob Stewart woke him and said, "Admiral, Alan Reclin was shot down. He was about twenty to thirty miles south of Hanoi. His wingman Clyde Barrett followed him down and said, he saw his chute hit the trees. We are nearly sure he landed safely. I'm not sure the Cong knows he's down.

"We have rangers going into that area to try and find him. They're good and I think he has a fifty-fifty chance."

Yates said, "Let's not notify his wife immediately. We'll know something within the week. No use her worrying herself to death. I know for a fact how close they are. I talked to Alan's dad, Paul Drake, and he told how they were the most in love couple he had ever known. They've been that way since early childhood."

"Very well, Admiral, I agree with you. Is he really married to Lara Grey?"

The admiral nodded and Stewart said, "No wonder he's so devoted. I saw that movie, *A Woman's Love* and told my wife as we left the studio that I was in love. She hit me on the arm."

"Yeah, she's a looker alright, but just as pretty on the inside."

***

Nin and Alan left about dark. Alan just followed as it was very dark. He wondered how Nin knew the way. Every so often Nin would stop with his hand in the air. They would listen for awhile then travel on. They rested every hour or so as they listened.

Towards morning they came to another village. Nin ducked into a straw hut, but Alan waited. Soon Nin came to the opening and motioned him to enter. There was a nice looking woman there that smiled at him. She was missing a front tooth that didn't do much for her beauty, but she was still nice looking.

She didn't speak English, but said something to Alan. Alan just smiled. Nin said, "She's going to feed us." As Alan looked at his rice he visualized bacon and eggs and smiled to himself.

Alan again prayed. The woman did not know what he was saying, but bowed reverently.

They stayed there that day and left when darkness moved in. Alan bowed and thanked the woman. She understood he was thanking her.

They never spoke when they traveled as both knew it could be dangerous. They went around two villages that day. Around two in the afternoon they came to a fruit tree. It looked like wild plums to Alan.

Alan asked, "Is the fruit alright to eat. Nin just hunched his shoulders and picked a couple and put one in his mouth. He quickly spat it out with a terrible look on his face, so Alan didn't pick any. He was starved and began looking at the vegetation around him as they traveled.

The terrain changed and they could see acres of rice paddies. Nin said, "I have an older sister who lives here. She will feed us. She likes American soldiers. She lived with one for awhile, then he left. Her husband was taken by the Vietcong, and hasn't been heard of for over three years. You will like her. She speaks English. She and her husband owned a lot of the rice paddies, and they are well off compared to the people around them.

"I've been trying to teach her about Jesus, but so far I haven't done so good with her. I'm hoping you can tell her in such a way that she will believe."

"I'm surely not good at that, but I will do my best. Maybe this is why I was sent here by Jesus."

Nin smiled and said, "I hope so. I love her and want her in heaven with me."

They came to a place that was much better than the surrounding huts. It had several rooms with nice furniture. Nin's sister was not there, but there was a place for Alan to bathe and he washed his flight suit and underwear at the same time. Nin hung out his clothes and gave him a white slip over robe to wear while waiting for everything to dry.

In the meantime, Nin found some things to eat. There was vegetables and some meat with their rice. Alan's stomach had shrunk so he still didn't eat much.

At dusk, a woman appeared and hugged Nin. She then saw Alan and bowed. He now was wearing his flight suit, so she knew he was an American flyer.

She left and bathed. She was gone sometime and when she appeared she was dress in a silk kimono. Her hair was done nicely and she was a beauty.

She said, "Welcome to my humble house. My name is Jinsi."

Alan said, "I'm called Alan. Your brother saved my life and I am eternally grateful. Thank you for taking me in."

She said, "I will fix you some food, and she turned to a room where cooking was done and disappeared. In about fifteen minutes she appeared again and with a smile said, "Diner is served."

They came into the room and a table was set with a table clothe and plates and silverware. Alan was astonished, and it must have shown, because Jinsi said, "My boyfriend brought these to me as he like to dine this way."

She had several vegetables and some pork.

Before they ate, Alan said, "Would you mind if I prayed over the food."

She smiled and said, "Please do."

Alan said, "Dear Lord you have led me to a beautiful house and a beautiful woman. Thank you for her hospitality.

Thank you again for Nin, who saved my life. Thank you for entering his body with your holy spirit so that he will spend eternity in heaven with me. Bless the food that Jinsi prepared for us and thank you for her. Bless her house and that she may receive your spirit and live forever in heaven with us. Amen."

Jinsi said, "You believe that a spirit entered you and Nin's body?"

"Yes, I know it did as I can feel the spirit and it guides me and keeps me safe. It is a wonderful feeling knowing you never have to be worried again about dying as you know you will be in heave with Jesus."

"My, Nin, you never told me that a spirit entered your body."

Nin said, "I forgot to tell you. The Holy spirit entered my body when I asked Jesus to come into my heart. He is with me at all times and I feel much safer."

She turned to Alan and said, "You must tell me more about this Jesus."

Alan said, "That is why Jesus sent me to Vietnam. I am married and love my wife dearly, but I am grateful that Jesus took me away from my home and brought me to Vietnam to tell you about Jesus. You see I would go to the ends of the world to tell you about what Jesus has for you."

Jinsi was wide eyed now. She said, "You believe this is why you came to Vietnam and were shot down?"

"Yes, I truly believe that Jesus brought me to your village here in Vietnam just to tell you about Jesus. I believe Jesus has written your name in his Book of Life. You must ask Jesus to forgive your sins and are sincere about that, then when you ask Jesus to come into your heart, he will forgive your sins and you will then follow him for the rest of your life.

"After Jesus comes into your heart, you will have the Holy Sprit in you forever.

"You will then have a place in heaven and no one can take that away."

"What if I sin again? I am prone to sin. Will he kick me out."

"No, when Jesus enters your heart, he forgives all the sins you have committed and all the sins you are going to commit. You see we are all human, and humans cannot keep from sinning. We try not to, but invariably we sin. However, he has forgiven all the sins that you will commit until you die."

She turned to Nin and said, "Why didn't you tell me all this Nin?"

"I truly didn't know it all. All I knew was that I wanted to follow Jesus the rest of my life. I don't know much, but I know that."

Alan said, "And that's enough, Nin. You understood the important part. Jesus forgave your sins that you confessed and you invited Jesus into your life."

Jinsi said, "I want to do that. I have sinned and I know it. I want to confess all my sins to Jesus and ask him to forgive me. I want that Holy spirit in me like you and Nin have. I must confess, I wanted to sleep with you tonight, but now I don't, so Jesus is already working on me. Will you help me?"

Alan said, "Are you truly sorry for the sins you have committed?"

Jinsi said, "Yes, now that I know the Holy Spirit will be in me, I don't want to sin in front of the Holy Spirit."

"Then ask Jesus to come into your heart and dwell with you forever."

"Come into my heart Lord Jesus."

Alan said, "You are the newest member of the heavenly host and will be with Nin and I in heaven."

Nin said, "The food is cold now, but you will be with me forever, Jinsi.

Jinsi reheated the food and it was a joyful meal.

Nin and Alan left the next evening. Before leaving Jinsi hugged Alan and said, "I hope you don't have to go to the North Pole for the next person, Alan. The Lord is surely using you."

They were on a trail that was wider. Nin said, "This trail will lead you to the ocean. I think the Cong has been run out of this area, so you should be safe. I'm going back to Jinsi. She will need me for a month or two. I feel the Lord wants me to help her."

"Then I think she should go. Try to tell others what you know about Jesus, Nin. I will never forget you and I will see you in heaven with Jinsi."

They parted with a hug.

CHAPTER 21

The Return Home

The trail to the ocean was not as easy as Nin thought it was. Jinsi had packed them a lot of food and Nin had left Alan with all he had. However, he was on the trail for two days and saw no end of it. He was now running out of food.

Alan passed three villages, but went around them as he didn't trust the Vietnamese, as they didn't really like the Americans or the Communist. They especially didn't like the war.

Alan finally had to chance it. He came to a village and spoke with their leader. The Communist had been brutal to their village and killed several men and raped their women. There was a woman who spoke English and interpreted for Alan.

Alan told the leader he had been shot down and was trying to get back to the American lines. The leader told them that a boat would be leaving in a few days to get supplies. Alan had not even seen the river. It was there, but vegetation was covering it.

They put him with an old woman who was nearly blind. Alan helped her and although she spoke no English he could tell she was grateful for his help.

He was now on a fishing boat and they spent a day and a half getting to the Ocean. They let him out in a small city that was in the hands of the Americans. He found a military installation and made contact with a Major Evans.

Major Evans called headquarters and Alan made contact with Admiral Yates. Yates said, "We were about to give up and tell your wife you were MIA, but I made them hold off. I surely didn't want to tell Betty Sue until we knew something concrete. I'm surely glad I waited."

"I am too, Admiral."

"I'm sending transportation for you immediately. Just sit tight. Let me talk to Major Evans again."

Alan handed the phone over. Evans said, "You bet, Admiral, I'll do that."

Evans smiled and said, "Is the Admiral your father?"

Alan smiled and said, "He is a little over protective. I've been with him sense Korea on the Princeton."

"Well, I'm to make sure you are guarded properly and have the best food available."

Alan smiled and said, "I'll tell him you did all that. All I want is a hamburger and a milkshake."

"I can do that Commander."

After meeting Admiral Yates, Alan had a hot shower, and slept in a good bed.

The Admiral said, "You are entitled to thirty days leave. I'm sending you home."

Alan said, "Don't tell anyone, I want to surprise Betty Sue."

Yates smiled and said, "Yeah, that will be best. I would like to see that meeting though."

Alan had the taxi drive just to the gate. He knew the gate code and walked to the house. He could hear splashing off the cliff and knew Betty Sue was swimming. He walked down the stairs and could see Betty Sue and Dorothy swimming. He took a chair as they were engrossed with their swimming. Betty Sue climbed the ladder and there sat Alan. She didn't scream. She just ran into his arms and cried. They held each other as Dorothy came up.

She just stood watching as they held each other. She said, "If I didn't know better, I would think you were newly weds.

THE END

Printed in the United States
By Bookmasters